February Frolics

Annie Seaton

The Enchanted Village: 3

Dedication

As always, to my love, Ian

Chapter One

The Village Waits

The first day of February dawned clear and cold over Lower Thistlewick, the kind of winter morning that made everything crisp and beautiful. Frost glittered on the village green; each blade edged with silver. The millstream flowed gently beneath the stone bridge, murmuring beneath the arch. Smoke rose from cottage chimneys in lazy spirals, and the air smelled of wood fires and frost still clinging to the ground.

Dimity Armstrong walked hand in hand with Vivian along the millstream path, both wrapped in thick coats, their breath making clouds in the cold air. They'd been together three months now, but Dimity still felt a thrill every time Vivian's fingers laced through hers.

'It's perfect today,' he said, stopping to look across the meadow where mist lingered in the hollows.

'The village looks like a painting.' Dimity squeezed his hand. 'That's part of its charm.'

They walked on, past Hawthorn Cottage where Joanna lived—lights on in the kitchen, smoke from the chimney suggesting she was up early baking. Past Lavender Cottage with its dormant garden waiting for spring. Past the Chapter & Verse bookshop, still dark at this hour, though Hugh Morrison would open it soon.

The village was small—barely two dozen cottages clustered around the green, the church with its Norman tower at one end, the pub at the other. But what this little village lacked in size, it made up for in character. Every cottage had a story. Every resident had been changed by living here. There was magic in the air, a magic that couldn't be explained but only felt.

'I can't believe we're staying here,' Dimity said as they approached the bridge.

'I'm happy,' Vivian said. 'No more commuting. Just here.'

'Having second thoughts?' Dimity kept her tone light. Vivian had come here from a reputable publishing house three months ago to help her edit her Shadowlands book, and sometimes, she still couldn't believe they had fallen in love. Now, they had decided to stay in the village in the house that Dimity had inherited.

'None at all.' Vivian stopped walking and turned to face her properly. 'This is where I want to be. Although if you decided to pack up and move to the outback, I'd follow you there too.'

'No chance of that,' she said with a grin. 'I love our village.'

They reached the bridge just as Hugh Morrison and Joanna Hartwell appeared from the other direction, clearly returning from their early morning walk to the top of the hill that overlooked the village. Hugh had his arm around Joanna's waist, and she was laughing at something he'd said, her face pink from the cold.

'Morning!' Hugh called out. 'You two are up early.'

'Couldn't sleep,' Dimity said, smiling. 'Too excited about everything. You?'

'Joanna wanted to see the sunrise over the meadow,' Hugh said. 'She's been sketching winter landscapes.'

'I have a new hobby,' Joanna added quickly. 'Just for myself. Learning watercolours.'

'They're beautiful,' Hugh said firmly. 'I think she should have an art show.'

Joanna flushed, and she shook her head, still shy in company. 'You're just biased, Hugh.'

'I'll be putting some in Chapter & Verse,' he said.

The four of them walked onto the bridge together, the traditional gathering spot for village chats. It was wide enough for people to stand and talk, with a low stone wall perfect for sitting. The millstream burbled beneath them, higher than usual after recent rain, and a robin appeared from somewhere to perch on the bridge rail, as if it wanted to be part of the conversation.

'So,' Hugh said, looking at Dimity and Vivian with interest. 'I hear you've decided to stay in the village.'

Dimity shook her head. 'Mrs

Willoughby? I swear that woman has telepathy. I didn't tell her.' She turned to Vivian. 'Did you?'

'No,' Vivian said, grinning. 'But yes, Hugh. We're permanent residents of Lower Thistlewick now. No more weekend visits. We're here for good.'

'That's wonderful!' Joanna hugged them both, her warmth genuine.

'The cottage practically decided for us,' Dimity said. 'That's how it felt, anyway. It might sound strange, but that's the way it was.'

'That's how Hawthorn Cottage feels to me,' Joanna agreed. 'Like coming home to a place I'd never been before.'

'And I'm very happy about that.' Hugh put his arm around Joanna's shoulder. 'We just have to hope that you'll decide to stay. too.'

Her smile was still shy, but Dimity could tell by Joanna's expression that she wouldn't be leaving Hugh and Emma. She was sure that their new relationship would strengthen and grow.

They stood together on the bridge, talking about the peculiarities of the village's cottages—how each one seemed to find exactly the right person, how they helped people heal and grow and become themselves. Dimity tried to imagine having this conversation with her parents in their little town of Yungaburra in Australia, but she knew it would sound like something from her stories. A conversation that would sound mad anywhere else, but here, in this village that believed in magic, it was perfectly normal.

'Well, I'd better go and open the shop,' Hugh said, holding his hand out to Joanna.

'Before you go, I have some news,' Dimity said, unable to keep the smile from her face any longer. 'Rather big news.'

Vivian was practically bouncing beside her. 'She does!'

Hugh and Joanna waited, looking at her curiously.

'Television. My stories are going to be on television. Netflix,' Dimity said, the words coming out in a rush. 'They've signed a contract for my Shadowlands series. All five books. They're making them into television shows. Five seasons already contracted. Worldwide distribution.'

The reaction was immediate and loud. Hugh let out a whoop that scattered the robin. Joanna shrieked and grabbed Dimity's hands. Vivian was beaming down at her, and Dimity was being hugged by everyone at once.

'That's incredible!' Hugh said. 'That's— Dimity, that's amazing! When did you find out?'

'I got a call late last night. We've been

sitting on it since I first arrived, and it took ages for Lila—my agent—to finalise the contract. She was amazing.' Dimity was grinning so widely her cheeks hurt. 'The contracts are signed now. Production starts in March. And the big news is…' She looked up at Vivian.

'They possibly will film some of it here. In the village,' he said, looking down at her proudly.

'Here?' Joanna looked around as if seeing Lower Thistlewick with new eyes. 'Our village? On Netflix?'

'They loved the setting when I described it to them. I wrote the first book here, and I guess it guided my descriptions when I was building my fantasy world. The stone bridge, the cottages, the millstream. They said it was perfect for the atmosphere they wanted.' Dimity leaned against the bridge wall, still slightly stunned by how much her life had changed.

'We'll have location scouts visiting in a few weeks. Nothing's guaranteed, but they're very interested.'

'This calls for a celebration,' Hugh said decisively. 'A proper celebration. Shall we meet at The Old Swan tonight? Drinks on me.'

The Old Swan was the village pub, officially named The Old Swan & Millstream but called The Old Swan by everyone local. It was warm and friendly, with low-beamed ceilings and a fire that burned year-round, run by publican Alf Cooper, who'd been pulling pints in the same location for thirty years.

'I'll bring champagne,' Vivian said. 'We've been saving a good bottle for exactly this.'

'I'll tell Alf to expect us,' Hugh said. 'He'll want to hear the news anyway. This is huge for the village. Netflix in Lower Thistlewick!'

They were still talking excitedly when a voice called from across the green.

'Well, well. What's all this commotion?'

They turned to see Iris Willoughby walking toward them, wrapped in a purple coat with a fox fur collar that had seen better days but which she wore with absolute panache. She was elderly—well into her eighties—but moved with the confidence of someone who'd lived in the same village her entire life and knew every stone of it.

'Mrs Willoughby!' Dimity called. 'We have news!'

They caught her up as she reached the bridge, and her face split into a delighted smile as Dimity explained about the Netflix deal.

'My dear girl, that's wonderful! Absolutely wonderful!' Mrs Willoughby beamed at them all, her eyes bright with pleasure. 'Such talented young people we have here. This village is blessed, truly blessed.'

She looked at each couple in turn—Dimity and Vivian with their linked hands, Hugh with his arm still around Joanna's waist—and her smile grew even wider.

'Two such happy couples,' she said warmly. 'It does my heart good to see it. Love is blooming in every corner of our village.'

There was something in her tone, something knowing and slightly mischievous, that made Dimity look at her more closely.

'You look like you know something we don't,' Vivian observed.

'I'm an old woman. I know many things.' Mrs Willoughby's eyes twinkled. 'But I do have a sense—call it intuition, call it village magic—that we'll be seeing more happy developments very soon. More joy coming to Lower Thistlewick.'

'That's wonderfully cryptic,' Hugh said,

amused. 'You should write stories.'

'I like to maintain an air of mystery, dear.' Mrs Willoughby patted his arm. 'It keeps me interesting. But mark my words—the village isn't done working its particular magic. Something lovely is coming. I can feel it in my bones.'

Before anyone could press her for details, footsteps approached from the village shop, and JK Jolie appeared carrying a basket. JK was in her sixties, elegant in a way that suggested French heritage, and she ran the village sweet shop with passionate attention to detail.

'*Bonjour*!' she called, her accent still pronounced despite thirty years in England. 'I bring offerings!' She held up the basket. 'Fresh madeleines, still warm. I was testing a new recipe, and I have far too many. You will help me, yes?'

'You're a saint,' Vivian said, accepting a madeleine and biting into it. 'Oh, that's perfect. What's in these?'

'Honey and lavender. A little experiment.' JK looked pleased. 'And what brings everyone to the bridge so early? Is there news?'

They told her about the Netflix deal, and JK's reaction was as enthusiastic as everyone else's. She insisted they must come to the shop later and choose their favourite sweets as a celebration—'on the house, naturally, for our village celebrity!'

'Hardly a celebrity,' Dimity protested.

'Netflix is Netflix,' JK said firmly. 'This is very big. The village will be so proud.'

Alf Cooper appeared next, walking from The Old Swan with his usual unhurried stride. He was a large man, barrel-chested, with a grey beard and the calm demeanour of someone who'd spent decades listening to other people's troubles while wiping down bar tops.

'Morning, all,' he said in his deep voice. 'JK, are those your madeleines? Save one for me.' He accepted the pastry she offered, then looked at the group assembled on the bridge. 'What's the occasion? You lot look like you're plotting something.'

'Netflix,' Hugh said simply.

'Netflix what?'

'Dimity's sold her books to Netflix. They're filming it. Might even be filmed here.'

Alf's eyebrows rose slowly. 'Well now. That is news.' He turned to Dimity. 'Congratulations, lass. Well deserved. Those books of yours are proper good. I've read them all.'

This surprised Dimity. Alf had never mentioned reading her work before. 'Really?'

'Course. We've got a bestselling author

in the village. I like to know what she's writing about.' He grinned. 'And the stories are cracking good. Can't put them down.'

'We're celebrating at The Old Swan tonight,' Hugh said. 'Will you join us?'

'I'll be behind the bar, won't I? But I'll toast you properly.' Alf looked at the group with satisfaction. 'Good to see people happy. The village has been quiet lately. Nice to have something to celebrate.'

'Mrs Willoughby thinks more good things are coming,' Vivian said. 'She says the village isn't done with its magic yet.'

'The village is always up to something,' Alf said sagely. 'Just when you think it's settled down, something new happens. Someone new arrives, or someone figures out what they've been missing, or a cottage decides it's time to help somebody.' He shrugged his massive shoulders. 'That's just how it is here. Magic's in the stones and the water and the air.'

They stood together on the bridge, sharing madeleines and talking about love and books and the peculiar enchantment of this place they called home. The sun climbed higher, burning off the frost, and the village began to properly wake. Lights came on in more cottages. Someone started playing piano—scales at first, then a recognisable melody drifted across the green.

'I should open the shop,' Hugh said eventually. 'Emma's probably waiting for me, but I promised I'd have tea ready when she gets back from feeding her gran's chickens.'

'And I need to sketch before I lose this light,' Joanna said. 'The way the frost is melting—it's perfect.'

They said their goodbyes with promises to meet at The Old Swan that evening, and slowly dispersed back to their various cottages and businesses. But Dimity and Vivian lingered on the bridge, watching the millstream flow beneath them.

'Are you really happy?' Vivian asked quietly. 'About all of it? The books, the movie, everything?'

'Happier than I've ever been.' Dimity pulled her close. 'Three years ago, when I stayed here and began to write, I was happy, but I was lonely. And now look at me. Books on Netflix. Living in a magical village with the man I love. Sometimes I can't quite believe it's real.'

'It's real.' Vivian kissed her temple. 'And you deserve every bit of it.'

'So do you. We both do.' Dimity looked around at the village, at the cottages and the green and the bridge that had witnessed so many important moments. 'Mrs Willoughby's right, you know. Something is coming. I can feel it too. The village has that waiting feeling. Like it's holding its breath.'

'Good something or bad something?'

'Good.' Dimity was certain. 'Definitely good. The village doesn't wait for bad things. It waits for people who need it. For stories that need telling. For magic that needs to happen. No wonder I can write so quickly here.'

They stayed on the bridge a little longer, wrapped in their coats and their happiness, watching the village come alive around them. And if they'd known that Emma Morrison would discover a girl with silver-blonde hair and flowers in her wake, sitting on this very bridge, reading a book and looking like something out of a fairy tale at dawn tomorrow —well, they might have smiled and nodded and said yes, that sounds exactly right.

The magic was always there, flowing like the millstream, constant as the stones in the bridge. You just had to be brave enough to believe in it, Dimity thought.

***

Emma Morrison crossed the bridge later that day, just as afternoon was fading to evening, her school bag bouncing on her back, her hair escaping from its ponytail. She'd spent the day at school in the neighbouring village, and the school bus had dropped her off at the lane entrance.

'Dimity! Vivian!' she called, spotting them still lingering near Pippin's Nook. 'Are you really staying? Dad told me at lunch! You're not leaving anymore?'

'We're really staying,' Dimity confirmed, catching Emma in a hug. 'Pippin's Nook is our permanent home now.'

'That's brilliant!' Emma was twelve, all energy and enthusiasm and opinion. 'I was worried you'd go back to London and we'd only see you on weekends. But now you'll be here all the time!'

'All the time,' Vivian agreed. 'You're stuck with us.'

'Good.' Emma grinned. 'Someone needs to keep an eye on you two. Make sure you're not getting into trouble.'

'We're the adults,' Dimity protested.

'Doesn't mean you have to behave.' Emma looked around the village, at the evening settling over the cottages, at lights coming on in windows. 'It's nice tonight, isn't it? Even though it's cold. There's something about February. Like winter's ending, but spring hasn't quite started. Everything's sort of waiting.'

'That's very poetic,' Vivian said.

'I get it from Mum.' Emma's expression softened for a moment—her mother had died four years ago, but she still talked about her often, keeping her memory alive through small mentions. 'She used to say February was the month for brave things. For making decisions. For taking steps you'd been too scared to take before.'

'Your mum sounds as though she was very wise,' Dimity said gently.

'She was.' Emma adjusted her school bag. 'I'm going to sit on the bridge for a bit. Read before dinner. Dad won't expect me for another hour, and I like it there when it's quiet.'

'Don't stay too late,' Vivian said. 'It gets cold once the sun's down.'

'I won't.'

Emma walked to the bridge and climbed up to sit on the wall, exactly where countless villagers had sat before her, her legs dangling over the millstream. She pulled a battered paperback from her bag—*The Wind in the Willows*, one of her mother's favourites—and opened it to a dog-eared page.

The millstream sang beneath her. The village settled into evening quiet. A robin appeared and hopped along the bridge rail, keeping her company as she read.

And if Emma noticed that the air felt particularly expectant tonight, that the village seemed to be full of anticipation, that something magic felt closer than usual—well, she was her mother's daughter. She knew magic when she felt it.

She just didn't know yet that tomorrow morning, at dawn, she would find something extraordinary waiting for her on the bridge. Someone extraordinary.

But that was tomorrow's magic.

Tonight, Emma read her book as the sun set, unaware that the village was holding its breath, waiting for a girl with flowers in her footsteps and fear in her heart to arrive and learn what the village had known all along:

That running away was just another path to coming home.

That love was braver than fear.

That magic was real if you believed in it.

Chapter Two

A Fairy on the Bridge

The next morning, Emma Morrison was crossing the old stone bridge on her way to feed Gran's chickens when she saw the girl.

She sat on the bridge wall with her legs dangling over the millstream, reading a book as if it were perfectly normal to be outside at dawn in February wearing only a thin dress covered in embroidered flowers. Her hair—so pale it was almost silver—was caught up in a messy braid with flowers—real flowers— tucked through it, and when she turned the page, the movement of her hands was so graceful that Emma's breath caught. Emma's eyes widened, and she dropped her chicken feed bucket. She put a hand to her mouth as a little gasp escaped.

The girl looked up, as if she'd felt Emma

watching, and smiled.

Emma stared at her. She had the most extraordinary eyes—grey-green like the millstream on a cloudy day—old soul eyes, but with a spark of pure mischief-making. She looked young, maybe early or mid-twenties, but also somehow timeless, as if she could have been sitting on that bridge for a hundred years, just waiting for the right person to notice her.

'Hello,' the girl said, and her voice sounded like the millstream itself—musical, constant, with perfect cadence. 'Lovely morning, isn't it?'

Emma managed a squeak that might have been agreement. She knew she could be friends with this girl. She just knew it without thinking.

'You're up early.' The girl marked her place in the book with a pressed violet and set it beside her on the stone. 'Feeding chickens?'

'Gran's chickens,' Emma said, finding her voice. 'How did you know?'

'The bucket rather gave it away.' The girl's smile widened. 'I'm Fern. I'm camping across the bridge for a few days. I hope that's all right.'

Emma's eyes widened. She looked past the bridge, past the girl, and there—just visible in the misty dawn light across the field—was a tent. Small, dome-shaped, the colour of morning mist itself, as if it had simply materialised out of the February fog.

'You're camping? Outside?' Emma breathed. 'In February?'

'It's not so cold if you don't mind it.' Fern swung her legs slightly, and Emma blinked. Her feet were bare. Actually *barefoot,* in February, as if frost and frozen ground meant nothing to her. 'I like the quiet of winter mornings. And your village is so beautiful.'

'Are you a fairy?' The question burst out before Emma could stop it.

To her credit, Fern didn't laugh. She tilted her head, considering the question seriously. 'What makes you think I might be?'

'You're sitting on our bridge in February with no shoes, and you're not cold. You have flowers in your hair even though it's winter. And there's a—' Emma gestured vaguely at the space around Fern, trying to find words for something she could feel but not quite see. 'There's a sparkly sort of feeling around you.'

'Ah.' Fern's expression was delighted. 'You're one who can see properly. How wonderful. So, yes! We can be friends.' She leaned forward conspiratorially. 'Can I tell you a secret?'

Emma nodded so hard her hairclip slid out.

'Whether I'm a fairy or not depends

entirely on whether you believe in them. Some people see magic everywhere. Others can't see it even when it's sitting right in front of them on a bridge.' Fern's smile was warm. 'What do you believe?'

'I believe,' Emma said immediately. 'This village has magic. Everyone knows it. The cottages help people, and flowers bloom at the wrong times, and sometimes things happen that can't be explained. And look at you with flowers in your hair.'

'Then I suppose I might be a fairy.' Fern picked up her book again. 'Or I might just be a girl who loves stories and didn't want to miss the sunrise. Perhaps both can be true at once.'

A robin landed on the bridge beside Fern and hopped across to settle on her knee as if they were old friends. It cocked its head at Emma, trilled once, then settled into Fern's palm when she offered it.

'Definitely a fairy,' Emma whispered to herself.

'Emma Morrison!' A voice called from across the green, and Emma turned to see her father emerging from their cottage, pulling on his coat. 'What are you doing on the bridge? Gran's waiting for those—'

He stopped dead when he saw Fern.

'Dad!' Emma ran to him, grabbed his hand, and dragged him toward the bridge. 'Dad, come meet Fern! She's camping in the field, and I think she's a fairy and she has a robin and—'

'Slow down, love.' Hugh let himself be pulled along, but his eyes were on Fern, who'd stood up from the bridge wall with fluid grace. The robin flew to her shoulder and stayed there, as comfortable as a tame bird. 'Good morning,' he said carefully. 'I'm Hugh Morrison. I own the bookshop.' He gestured back toward

Chapter & Verse. 'My daughter seems to think you're a fairy.'

'Your daughter knows how to look properly.' Fern stepped off the bridge wall onto the lane, and Hugh noticed that despite being barefoot, her feet weren't dirty or scraped or even particularly cold-looking. 'I'm Fern Rowan. I'm travelling through, and I was hoping I might camp in the field for a few days. Is that allowed? I asked the field very nicely, and it didn't seem to object.'

'You asked the field,' Hugh repeated, slowly shaking his head.

'Well, yes. It's polite to ask before you take up space somewhere, don't you think?' Fern's expression was perfectly serious, but something in her eyes suggested she was testing him. Seeing if he was someone who could play along or someone who would insist on being sensible about everything.

Hugh had lived in this village long enough to know when to let go of common sense.

'I suppose the field is public land,' he said. 'Though it's February. It's freezing. Do you have proper camping equipment? A good sleeping bag?'

'Oh, I don't feel the cold much.' Fern waved a hand dismissively. 'I'm quite comfortable, I promise. I have everything I need.'

'What are you reading?' Emma asked, bouncing on her toes, desperate to get back to the interesting bits.

Fern held up the book—a battered copy of *The Wind in the Willows*. 'I'm rereading an old friend. I like to read a chapter each morning before the world properly wakes up.'

'That's one of my favourites! I read it on the bridge just yesterday!' Emma's face lit up.

'Dad reads it at story time sometimes, too.'

'Storytime?' Fern's whole demeanour brightened. 'You have story times here? In the village?'

'Saturday mornings. In the bookshop,' Hugh said. 'For the village children, and visitors. Sometimes grown-ups come too. Nothing fancy, just—'

'That sounds wonderful.' Fern clutched the book to her chest, and for a moment, she looked less like a fairy and more like someone who lived for stories. 'I love stories. I'm actually—well, I was—I'm taking a break from university. English literature. But I love reading to children. It's the most magical thing, watching them believe in the story completely.'

Hugh studied her. Up close, he could see she was younger than he'd first thought. Pretty in an ethereal, otherworldly way that reminded him uncomfortably of the fairy tales Emma loved. Silver-blonde hair, grey-green eyes, a face that was all angles and light. But it was her enthusiasm that caught him. The way she lit up talking about stories.

'Would you like to do a reading?' he asked without thinking. 'At the bookshop? We're always looking for guest readers.'

'Really?' Fern's smile was luminous. 'I'd love to read. I'd read for free. For the joy of it.'

'We don't pay our readers,' Hugh said. 'It's a volunteer community thing.' He paused. 'Are you sure you're all right camping? It's meant to rain later this week.'

'I'll be fine.' Fern's confidence was absolute. 'The tent is waterproof, and I don't mind a bit of rain. Honestly, Mr Morrison, I've been camping since I was a child. I'm quite hardy.'

The robin on her shoulder chirped

agreement, and Hugh found himself smiling despite his concerns.

'All right. But if you need anything—food, warmth, a place out of the rain, anything—the bookshop is open six days a week. Come find me. You will be welcomed.'

'That's very kind.' Fern's expression softened. 'Truly. You're a good person, aren't you? I can always tell.'

Before Hugh could respond to that odd statement, Emma grabbed Fern's hand. 'Can you read today? This afternoon? Please? I'll tell everyone!'

'Emma, she just arrived—'

'I'd be delighted,' Fern interrupted. 'What time?'

'Three o'clock?' Hugh suggested, giving in to the inevitable. When Emma got an idea, there was no stopping her. And having a guest reader would be nice. Joanna had suggested the bookshop needed more community involvement anyway. Not that Fern was part of the community, but she had offered.

'Perfect.' Fern squeezed Emma's hand. 'I'll bring my favourite stories. The magical ones.'

'The magical ones are the best ones,' Emma said seriously.

'The only ones worth reading, really.' Fern winked, and the robin flew from her shoulder to circle both her and Emma once before darting off toward the trees.

Hugh watched it go, then looked back at Fern, who was already returning to her perch on the bridge wall, book in hand, as if this entire conversation had been a pleasant interlude, but now it was time to get back to the important business of reading by a millstream at dawn.

'Come on, Em,' he said. 'Gran's waiting for those chickens to be fed. I'll come with you and have a cup of tea with her.'

Emma waved enthusiastically at Fern, who waved back without looking up from her book, and allowed her father to lead her across the green towards her grandmother's cottage.

'She's definitely a fairy,' Emma said as they walked. 'Definitely, definitely.'

'She's a literature student on a camping trip,' Hugh corrected gently.

'She can be both.' Emma had inherited her mother's logic, and Hugh knew that Sarah had never let logic get in the way of wonder. 'Magic doesn't have to make sense, Dad. It just has to be believed in.'

Hugh looked back at the bridge. Fern was silhouetted against the rising sun, her silver hair catching the light, the millstream flowing beneath her, and for just a moment, Hugh could see what Emma saw. Something not quite of this world.

Then Fern turned a page, the mundane gesture breaking the spell, and she was just a girl reading on a bridge on a February morning.

Just a girl.

By nine o'clock, the entire village knew about the fairy in the field.

Hugh heard it three times at the shop. Margaret from The Cosy Cup came in to ask if he'd seen the "peculiar young woman camping". The young barman, Tom from the pub, mentioned that "some hippie" had set up a tent. And Mrs Pemberton, who ran the village shop with her sister, wanted to know if "that poor dear" needed anything.

'She's fine,' Hugh said for the third time. 'She's a literature student. She's camping for a few days. And yes, I've spoken to her. She seems perfectly capable.'

'In February?' Mrs Pemberton shook her head. 'She'll catch her death.'

'She says she doesn't feel the cold.'

'Well, that's not natural, is it?'

Hugh refrained from pointing out that approximately seventy percent of what happened in this village wasn't strictly natural and returned to cataloguing the new books that had arrived in an order this morning.

The day passed in the usual rhythm of a Monday at Chapter & Verse. A few browsers, a couple of sales, the comfortable quiet of a bookshop in winter. Hugh had just put the kettle on for afternoon tea when the door chimed, and Fern walked in.

She'd put on shoes—simple canvas trainers—and added a cardigan over the flower-covered dress, but she still looked like someone who had wandered out of a watercolour painting.

Joanna would love her, he thought.

The robin was perched on her shoulder

again, which was odd enough that Hugh blinked.

'That bird really likes you,' he said.

'We're old friends.' Fern didn't elaborate. 'Is it still all right if I read this afternoon? I know Emma was excited, but I wanted to check you hadn't changed your mind.'

'Not at all. We're expecting about a dozen children, maybe more if word has spread.' Hugh gestured around the shop. 'We usually set up cushions by the fireplace. Nothing formal.'

'Perfect.' Fern drifted toward the shelves, running her fingers along the spines with obvious reverence. 'You have a beautiful shop. It feels loved.'

'Twenty years of accumulation,' Hugh said. 'It was my father's before it was mine.'

'Books remember being loved.' Fern

pulled out a volume—a children's illustrated edition of *Alice in Wonderland*—and opened it carefully. 'This one's been read so many times. You can tell. The spine's soft, the pages are turned at the corners. Someone adored this.'

'My daughter,' Hugh admitted. 'When she was younger. Before...' He stopped, surprised at himself. He didn't usually share Sarah's death with strangers.

But Fern just nodded, seeming to understand without him having to explain. 'I'm sorry. Loss leaves a feeling in places, doesn't it? But so does love. And there's much more love than loss here.' She replaced the book gently. 'You've built something good. Stories and warmth and a place people can rest. That's a kind of magic too.'

Before Hugh could respond, the door chimed again, and Joanna came in, cheeks pink from the cold.

'Hugh, Mrs Pemberton said there's a—oh.' She stopped, seeing Fern. 'Hello. I'm Joanna. I live at Hawthorn Cottage, just down the way.'

'Fern Rowan.' Fern's smile was warm. 'I'm camping in the field. I'm also reading stories this afternoon if you'd like to come.'

'I'm a bit old for story time,' Joanna said with a laugh.

'No one's too old for stories.' Fern's expression was serious despite her light tone. 'Stories are how we remember how to be human. How to be kind. How to believe in good things.'

Joanna and Hugh exchanged glances, and Hugh saw his own thoughts reflected in Joanna's expression: this girl was unusual. Different in a way this village understood.

'I'll come,' Joanna said. 'If that's all right.'

'The more the merrier.' Fern glanced at the clock on the wall. 'Two hours. That gives me time to choose the perfect story.' She wandered deeper into the shop, the robin still on her shoulder, and began pulling books from shelves with the confidence of someone who knew exactly what she was looking for.

Hugh made tea. Joanna helped him set up cushions by the fireplace, and as they worked, she spoke quietly.

'She's unusual, that girl.'

'You noticed too.' Hugh arranged the last cushion. 'Emma's convinced she's a fairy.'

'She might be.' Joanna's tone was matter-of-fact. 'There's something fey about her. Otherworldly. Ethereal. Like she's only half-here.' She paused, watching Fern across the shop, surrounded by books. 'She looks like she's stepped out of a Waterhouse painting. All that silver hair and those grey-green eyes. The flowers. The robin.'

Hugh knew the paintings Joanna meant—he'd sold enough art books to recognise the reference. Women in flowing dresses, surrounded by nature, half-wild and wholly magical. Ophelia among the flowers. The Lady of Shalott in her boat.

'She's running from something,' Hugh said quietly.

'Yes.' Joanna met his eyes. 'I recognise that look. I had it when I arrived.'

'You did. And the village helped you.'

'It did.' Joanna squeezed his hand. 'Maybe it'll help her too. If she lets it.'

As they spoke quietly, Fern sat cross-legged on the floor, surrounded by a growing pile of children's books, humming something that might have been a lullaby or might have been the gently burble of the millstream, and looking perfectly at home.

At three o'clock, the children began to arrive.

Emma came first, of course, dragging two school friends with her. Then more trickled in—the Pemberton twins, little Jack Fletcher, Maya Morrison from Hugh's cousin's side of the family, children from the village and from the neighbouring farms. They arranged themselves on cushions in a semi-circle, wide-eyed and expectant.

Joanna and Hugh stood at the back of the shop, and Hugh was surprised to see Dimity and Vivian slip in as well, Vivian's hand in Dimity's, both of them smiling.

'Wouldn't miss this,' Dimity whispered to Hugh. 'Emma said there was a fairy at the bookshop.'

'A literature student,' Hugh corrected automatically.

'Same thing, sometimes,' Vivian

murmured, and Hugh couldn't argue with that.

Fern had settled herself in a wingback chair Hugh had positioned near the fire. The robin had flown up to perch on the mantelpiece, watching proceedings like a particularly attentive audience member. Fern held a book in her lap, but Hugh noticed she hadn't opened it yet. She was just looking at the children, her expression soft and wondering, as if they were the magical thing, not her.

'Hello,' she said, and her voice carried perfectly despite being barely above a conversational volume. 'My name is Fern, and I love stories. Has anyone here ever heard a story that felt like magic?'

Every hand went up.

'Good.' Fern's smile widened. 'Because today we're going to read a story that is magic. Or maybe it's just a very good story, and we'll make the magic by believing in it together.

Sometimes it's hard to tell the difference.'

She opened the book—*The Velveteen Rabbit*—and began to read.

Hugh's breath caught. Beside him, Joanna's hand slipped into his and squeezed—once, twice—as if to confirm she was seeing it too. Fern didn't just read the words. She brought them to life. When she read about the Velveteen Rabbit, the children saw him. When she read about the nursery, they were there. Her voice changed for different characters, but it was more than that. The air in the shop seemed to shift, to become warmer, richer, filled with something that felt very much like love.

By the time she reached the part where the Rabbit becomes Real, Hugh noticed that several parents blinked away tears. Emma was clutching her knees to her chest, riveted. And even Vivian—who Hugh had always thought of as rather stoic—had suspiciously bright eyes as he put his arm around Dimity's shoulder.

When Fern closed the book, the silence lasted several long heartbeats. Then Emma started whistling, and everyone clapped, and Fern smiled—just a girl who loved stories, pleased that they'd enjoyed one—and the spell broke gently, leaving only warmth behind.

'Can you read another?' a small voice asked. Jack Fletcher, Hugh noticed with disbelief. One of the rough and tumble boys from the north end of the village.

'Tomorrow,' Fern promised. 'If you'd like. Same time?'

A chorus of yeses filled the bookshop.

The parents arrived gradually, collecting children who were still buzzing with excitement about the story. Fern stood by the door, thanking each family as they left, until only a few stragglers remained.

Dimity approached first, Vivian close

behind. 'That was extraordinary,' Dimity said, offering her hand. 'I'm Dimity March. This is my partner, Vivian.'

'Fern Rowan.' Fern shook both their hands, then paused. 'Dimity March—the author? I adore your *Shadowlands* books.' Her voice went shy. 'I've read them all.'

Dimity's face lit up. 'You have? That's wonderful. All the more reason you should come to tea.'

'We live at Pippin's Nook, just across the green.' Vivian smiled. 'Would you come tomorrow? I think you and Dimity would have a lot to talk about.'

'I'd like that,' Fern said, and she sounded like she meant it

'After you do story time?' Vivian suggested. 'I'll make something sweet.'

'Perfect.'

Joanna was next, pulling on her coat but

lingering by the fireplace. 'Fern, I was wondering—would you come to dinner with me at Hawthorn Cottage? Friday evening? Nothing fancy, just... I'd like to get to know you properly.'

'That's very kind.' Fern tucked a strand of hair behind her ear. 'I'd love to.'

'Seven o'clock, then.' Joanna smiled and headed for the door, then paused. 'Hugh's right, you know. You have a real gift.'

After she left, Emma barrelled into Fern with the full force of a twelve-year-old's enthusiasm, wrapping her arms around Fern's waist and squeezing tight.

'That was the best story ever,' Emma said, her voice muffled against Fern's cardigan. 'You're the best. Can you read tomorrow too? Please?'

Fern hugged her back and didn't let go right away. 'Same time tomorrow.'

'Promise?'

'Promise.'

Emma pulled away, grinned up at her, then ran to collect her school bag. 'Come on, Dad! Close up. We need to get home for dinner!'

'I'll be along in a minute,' Hugh called after her. 'Wait by the door.'

Emma rolled her eyes but obeyed, and suddenly the shop was quiet as Hugh stood by the dying fire.

Fern was replacing books on shelves, humming that millstream song again.

'That was remarkable,' Hugh said.

'They were a wonderful audience.' Fern slid *The Velveteen Rabbit* back into its place. 'Children always are. They believe so completely. Adults have to work at it, but children just... jump in.'

'Where did you learn to read like that?'

'My mother.' Fern's expression went distant, fond. 'She read to me every night when I was small. Made every story feel like it was happening right there in our sitting room. I suppose I learned from her.' She paused. 'She died when I was fifteen. But I still hear her voice when I read. Still feel her there.'

'I'm sorry,' Hugh said, understanding.

'Don't be. She gave me the best gift— she taught me how to keep stories alive.' Fern turned to face him properly. 'Thank you for letting me read, Mr Morrison. It means more to me than you know.'

'Hugh. Please.'

'Hugh, then.' Fern collected her cardigan from where she'd draped it over a chair. 'I should go before it gets dark. Let my tent know I'm coming back.'

'Does it worry you if you're late?' Hugh asked, deciding to meet her where she was.

'Everything worries if you're late and don't tell them where you've gone.' Fern's smile was luminous. 'Tents, plants, people who love you. It's only polite to let them know you're safe.'

She was at the door when Hugh called after her. 'Fern? Why are you really here? In our village?'

She turned back, silhouetted against the fading afternoon light, and for a moment, her expression was unguarded. Sad and hopeful and frightened all at once.

'Because I'm running away from something very important,' she said quietly. 'And I needed to remember why running away is always the wrong choice. I hope your village might help me remember.'

Before Hugh could ask what she was running from, she was gone, past Emma, and the door chimed gently behind her, the robin flying after her like a shadow.

Emma appeared at Hugh's elbow, watching through the window as Fern crossed the green.

'She's definitely a fairy,' Emma said matter-of-factly.

'Emma—'

'I know, I know. You're going to say she's just a girl who's camping and likes stories.' Emma turned to look up at him. 'But fairies can be those things too, Dad. Mum used to say that magic was just real life, but more so. More true. More itself.'

Hugh looked out at the green where Fern was disappearing towards her tent, the robin still following.

'She did say that, didn't she?'

'All the time.' Emma grabbed her school bag. 'And Fern's running from something important. That's what people do when they come here, right? They're running from things. And then the village helps them stop running.'

'How do you know that?'

Emma shrugged. 'Because it helped Joanna. And it helped Dimity and Vivian. And it's helping Fern now, even if she doesn't know it yet.' She headed for the door. 'Come on, Dad. Gran's making shepherd's pie, and if we're late she'll eat all the crispy bits.'

Hugh stood in his bookshop, surrounded by stories and the lingering warmth of a reading that had felt like magic, and thought about what Emma had said that morning.

Magic doesn't have to make sense. It just has to be believed in.

Three doors down, Mrs Willoughby stood at her window and watched Fern disappear into the mist-coloured tent. She smiled, satisfied.

'So,' she said to the empty room, 'she's

finally found her way here. About time.'

Here she was, sleeping in a tent in February because dramatic gestures ran in the family, reading stories to enchanted children, leaving flowers in her wake whether she knew it or not. Running from a boy who loved her. Running from the fear of choosing happiness.

'Well,' Mrs Willoughby said, putting the kettle on, 'let's see what the village can do with you, shall we, my dear?'

Outside, Fern's tent glowed softly from within, warm despite the February cold.

And on the stone bridge over the millstream, where a girl had sat at dawn reading about water rats and moles and the wild wood, a perfect circle of snowdrops bloomed in defiance of the season.

Magic, the village seemed to whisper. Or just a very good story, believed in completely.

Sometimes it was impossible to tell the

difference. And sometimes, that was exactly the point.

Chapter Three

The Village Adopts a Fairy

Fern woke on Tuesday morning to frost on her tent and a robin singing from the bridge.

She unzipped the tent flap and looked around as she stretched. The village had been transformed by overnight cold—everything was white and sparkling, the millstream smoking in the frigid air, her breath making clouds. It should have been miserable. She should have been frozen.

Instead, she felt perfectly comfortable, as if the February chill was just an interesting weather phenomenon that happened to other people.

'That's not normal,' she told the robin, who cocked his head as if to say, 'And your point is?'

She dressed quickly—the same flower-covered dress she'd worn yesterday, a cardigan, her canvas shoes—and stepped out of her tent just as the sun peeked above the hills. The village was still asleep, smoke rising from chimneys, curtains drawn. Only the robin and the millstream kept her company.

Fern walked to the bridge and sat on the wall, exactly where Emma had found her. She pulled out her book—still *The Wind in the Willows*, still her mother's battered copy—and tried to read. But the words blurred, and instead she found herself thinking about Callum.

Four days. It had been four days since she'd run. Four days since he'd asked her to marry him, and she'd panicked and disappeared. Four days of silence from her, although he had tried to call her. Tried to text. Tried to reach her in every way possible.

And she'd turned off her phone and run

to the countryside like a character in a novel, dramatic and more than a little ridiculous.

'What's wrong with me?' she asked the robin.

The robin had no answers, only more singing.

'Talking to birds now?'

Fern jumped, nearly dropping her book. Joanna stood at the end of the bridge, wrapped in a thick coat, holding two travel mugs.

'I brought tea,' Joanna said, offering one. 'Hugh said you'd be up early. He said you were here yesterday at dawn too.'

'I like mornings.' Fern accepted the tea gratefully. 'And the bridge. It's peaceful.'

'It is.' Joanna climbed up to sit beside her, legs dangling over the millstream. 'Though it's freezing. How are you not cold?'

'I don't really feel cold. Never have felt it.'

'That's the fairy thing Emma was talking about.'

'I'm not a fairy.' But Fern was smiling.

'If you say so.' Joanna sipped her tea, watching the millstream. 'I wanted to apologise, actually. For yesterday. At the reading. I cried all over your beautiful story.'

'*The Velveteen Rabbit* makes everyone cry. That's its job.'

'It was perfect. The way you read it. Like you were living every word.' Joanna glanced at Fern. 'You must love stories very much.'

'They're the only magic that's real,' Fern said, then reconsidered. 'Or maybe they're the only real thing that's also magic. I'm not sure which.'

They sat in comfortable silence for a while, watching the village wake up. Lights appeared in windows. A dog barked somewhere. The Cosy Cup's door opened, releasing the smell of fresh bread.

'Can I ask you something?' Joanna said eventually. 'You don't have to answer if it's too personal.'

'Go ahead.'

'Yesterday, when Hugh asked why you were really here, you said you were running from something important. Was it a person?'

Fern's hands tightened on her mug. 'Yes.'

'Someone you love?'

'Yes.'

'Someone who hurt you?'

'No. Someone I'm terrified of hurting. Someone I'm terrified of disappointing.' Fern took a shaky breath. 'Someone who asked me to marry him, and I said I needed to think about it, and then I ran away to live in a tent because apparently I handle emotional intimacy like a frightened rabbit.'

'Oh.' Joanna's voice was warm with understanding. 'I see.'

'Do you think I'm awful?'

'I think you're scared. There's a difference.' Joanna shifted to face Fern properly. 'Can I tell you about my parents?'

Fern nodded.

'They both died last year. Six months apart. I spent two years caring for them, watching them fade, knowing there was nothing I could do except be present.' Joanna's eyes were bright with unshed tears. 'And when they were gone, I realised I'd spent so long being a caregiver that I'd forgotten how to be anything else. I didn't know who I was without someone to look after.'

'That must have been terrible.'

'It was. So, I came here, to this village my mother had always loved. And Hawthorn Cottage—it taught me something.' Joanna smiled. 'It taught me that I was allowed to have my own life. My own joy. My own love. That giving yourself to others is beautiful, but so is receiving. So is being loved back.'

'What does that have to do with me?'

'Because I think you're doing the opposite. You're so afraid of taking up space, of being too much, of asking for love, that you run away from it.' Joanna touched Fern's hand gently. 'But love isn't a burden, Fern. Being loved isn't selfish. It's just... human.'

Fern lifted her hand and wiped away the tears that began to roll down her cheeks. 'What if I'm not enough? What if I marry him and he realises I'm just a strange girl who grows flowers accidentally and talks to birds and can't function in normal society?'

'Then he's an idiot. But I'm sure he's not.' Joanna squeezed her hand. 'I think he already knows exactly who you are. And that's why he wants to marry you.'

They sat together on the bridge until the tea grew cold, until the village was fully awake, until Emma appeared running across the green shouting, 'Fern! Fern! Can you read again today? Please?'

***

That afternoon's reading was even better attended than the first. Word had spread—a girl was camping in the field; a girl who read like she was spinning magic, and everyone wanted to see for themselves.

Fern read chapters from *The Secret Garden* this time, about a girl who was thorny, difficult, and unloved until she found a place where she could grow. About gardens that came back to life with attention and care. About the magic of believing things could get better.

When she finished, an unfamiliar woman approached. She was elderly, white-haired, with a certain authority.

'That was lovely, dear,' the woman said. 'I'm Iris Willoughby. I live in the cottage by the church.'

'Fern Rowan.' They shook hands.

Mrs Willoughby patted Fern's hand. 'Well, dear, you're very welcome here. Stay as long as you need. The village has a way of helping people figure out what they're running from and whether they should keep running or turn around.'

After she left, Hugh appeared at Fern's elbow. 'Mrs Willoughby doesn't usually come to story time. You've made an impression.'

Hugh watched Mrs Willoughby's retreat with a thoughtful expression.

***

Later in the afternoon, Fern accepted Dimity's invitation to tea at Pippin's Nook.

The cottage was warm and cluttered in

70

the best way—books piled on every surface, artwork on the walls, a cat sleeping in a basket by the fire. Dimity and Vivian moved around each other comfortably; their happiness showed in everything they said.

'We've been together three months,' Dimity explained, pouring tea. 'Vivian came here to edit my book after I'd had an accident.'

'Took her long enough to figure it out,' Vivian added, fond despite the teasing.

'I was terrified when we fell in love,' Dimity said simply. 'Of disappointing him. Of being different. Of admitting who I really was.' She looked at Fern directly. 'I wasted time being scared, Fern. Don't make my mistake.'

'I don't know how to stop being scared,' Fern admitted.

'You don't stop. You just choose to do the thing anyway.' Vivian set a plate of homemade biscuits on the table. 'That's what brave means. Not the absence of fear. Just doing the right thing despite it.'

They talked for a long time. The sun disappeared, and firelight lit the room as Dimity reassured her. About love and fear and the courage it took to be honest about who you were and what you wanted. About running away and coming back. About the village and its magic—how it seemed to draw people who needed to learn something essential about themselves.

'Why do you think I'm here?' Fern asked.

'To learn you're lovable,' Dimity said immediately. 'That's usually what the village teaches people. That they deserve happiness.'

When Fern walked back to her tent under moonlight, flowers had appeared along the path. Just a few—violets in the grass, primroses near the bridge. She stopped, stared at them, and touched one gently.

They were real. She'd grown them without meaning to, without trying. Just by walking, by being herself.

'Great,' she muttered to the flowers. 'Now everyone will definitely think I'm a fairy.'

But secretly, deep down, she was starting to think maybe being a fairy—being magical, being strange, being herself—wouldn't be the worst thing in the world.

Maybe it was exactly what she was supposed to be.

***

Wednesday brought rain.

Fern woke to the sound of it pattering on her tent, steady and relentless. She should have been miserable; camping in February rain should have been miserable. But her tent stayed dry, and she stayed warm, and when she emerged, the rain didn't seem to touch her.

'Definitely a fairy,' Emma declared when she found Fern on the bridge at dawn, reading in the rain without an umbrella and not getting wet. 'Normal people get soaked. You're completely dry.'

'The rain just... misses me.' Fern looked up at the clouds. 'It always has. I don't know why.'

'Because you're magic.' Emma sat beside her, under her own umbrella. 'Why won't you just admit it?'

'Because magic isn't real.'

'You're sitting in a village where cottages heal people and flowers bloom when they shouldn't and people find exactly what they need exactly when they need it, and you're still saying magic isn't real?'

Fern laughed despite herself. 'Well, when you put it that way...'

'I'm very logical.' Emma was serious. 'Dad says I get it from Mum. She was always logical, even about impossible things. She said logic and magic weren't opposites—they were just different ways of understanding the world.'

'She sounds wise.'

'She was.' Emma's expression went sad. 'She got sick and died when I was eight. But I remember her. How she read stories, how she made everything seem possible, how she never dismissed things just because they didn't make sense.'

'I'm sorry,' Fern said softly.

'It's okay. Well, not okay. But better now. Dad's happy again—he and Joanna are perfect together. I really hope they get married, but I'm going to let them decide that for themselves.'

'That's very wise of you,' Fern said gently.

Emma beamed. 'And I have Gran, and the village, and now I have you for a little while.' She looked at Fern hopefully. 'You are staying a while, right? Not leaving soon?'

'Not for a while,' Fern promised.

Until I sort out what I need to do.

Until maybe the villages teaches me what I need to do.

***

The rain continued all day, but it didn't stop people from coming to the afternoon reading. Chapter & Verse filled with villagers seeking warmth and stories, and Fern read *Paddington Bear*—about a small bear far from home, who found a family by simply being himself, marmalade sandwiches and all.

The children loved it. The adults loved it more. And Fern understood, finally, why stories mattered so much. They were mirrors and maps all at once. Showing you who you were, showing you where you might go.

That evening, she made a decision.

She couldn't call Callum—her phone was dead, left deliberately uncharged at her flat three hours away. But she could write to him. She could put words on paper, and could try to explain what she was learning here in this special village.

She sat in her tent with a notebook and pen she'd bought at the village shop, and she wrote:

Dear Callum,

I'm sorry. I'm so, so sorry for running. You deserve better than a silly woman who disappears into the countryside for weeks when things get scary.

I'm in a village called Lower Thistlewick. It's magic here—real magic, the kind you have to see to believe. Cottages that help people, flowers that bloom when they shouldn't, a bridge that feels like a threshold between worlds.

I've been learning things. About courage and fear and the difference between them. About running away versus running toward. About whether I deserve to be happy (the village says yes, even when I'm not convinced).

I don't know when I'm coming back. But I needed you to know I'm safe. I'm figuring things out. I'm trying to be brave enough to deserve you.

I love you. I'm sorry it's taken me so long to say it properly, to mean it without fear attached. But I do. I love you.

Give me a little more time. I promise I'll come back. And when I do, I'll give you an answer to your question.

Yours   (always),

Fern

She sealed it in an envelope, addressed it

to his flat, and left it on the counter at the village shop for posting tomorrow.

It wasn't calling him. It wasn't brave enough. But it was a start.

***

Thursday morning, Fern woke to find the rain had stopped and the flower path had tripled in size.

Violets, primroses, and now snowdrops—all blooming in a clear trail from her tent to the bridge and back. Evidence of her nightly walks, her pacing, her thinking.

The entire village came out to look.

'It's extraordinary,' Mrs Pemberton breathed. 'In the middle of winter.'

'It's a sign,' Margaret from The Cosy Cup declared. 'The village approves of her.'

'It's just flowers,' Fern tried to say, but no one was listening.

By noon, visitors from neighbouring

villages had started arriving to see the fairy girl's flower path. By afternoon, Fern was hiding in Chapter & Verse, overwhelmed by the curiosity.

'This is what happens when you're magic in a village that believes in magic,' Hugh said, amused. 'They celebrate it.'

'I just want to be left alone to read and think.'

'Then you came to the wrong village.' But Hugh's expression was kind. 'Though if you want actual advice—listen. Accept who you are. The village isn't going to stop believing you're magical just because you're uncomfortable with it.'

'What if I don't know what I am?'

'Then figure it out. You've got time. Your tent isn't going anywhere, and neither is the village.'

***

That afternoon, instead of reading at the bookshop, Fern walked along the millstream to think.

The flower path followed her, growing as she walked. She stopped fighting it, stopped trying to suppress whatever this was. And the more she relaxed, the more flowers appeared— not just three types now, but dozens. Early crocuses in purple and gold, tiny narcissus, even some early tulips that shouldn't appear in February.

She reached the meadow beyond the village and sat in the grass, surrounded by impossible blooms, and finally let herself cry.

For the six days she'd wasted running. For the fear that had ruled her for so long. For the mother she'd lost who would have understood this magic, who had probably lived with the same gift. For Callum, waiting at home, not knowing if she was coming back.

The robin appeared and settled on her knee. Fern stroked its feathers and let herself grieve for the girl she'd been—the one who thought being strange meant being unwanted, who thought magic was a curse, who thought love was something other people deserved but not her.

'I want to be different,' she told the robin. 'I want to be brave. I want to go home and say yes and mean it without fear.'

The robin chirped, which she chose to interpret as encouragement.

Chapter Four

Tea with Mrs Willoughby

Thursday afternoon brought an invitation Fern hadn't expected.

'Mrs Willoughby would like you to come for tea,' Emma announced, appearing at Fern's tent on her way back from her morning reading on the bridge. 'She sent me specially to ask. She says four o'clock, if you're free.'

'I don't want to impose—' Fern started.

'She doesn't ask people to tea unless she really wants them there,' Emma said seriously. 'It's an honour. You should go.'

So, at four o'clock, Fern found herself walking up the path to Iris Willoughby's cottage by the church. It was a proper Cotswold cottage—honey-coloured stone, climbing roses (dormant now but clearly magnificent in summer), and windows that looked like they'd been watching the village for centuries.

Mrs Willoughby opened the door before Fern could knock. 'Punctual. I like that. Come in, dear. The kettle has just boiled.'

The cottage interior was exactly what Fern had imagined—low beams, a fireplace with a crackling fire, furniture that had been here for decades, and photographs everywhere. It was strange, but she felt immediately at home; it was familiar. Photographs on the mantelpiece, on side tables, and covering an entire wall near the stairs.

'Family,' Mrs Willoughby said, catching Fern's gaze. 'Generations of us. I'm the last one living in the village now, but I like to keep them all close.' She gestured to a comfortable armchair by the fire. 'Sit. I'll bring the tea.'

Fern sat, feeling the chair embrace her. She looked up, examining the photographs while Mrs Willoughby bustled in the kitchen. Black and white images of stern Victorians. Sepia-toned wedding photos. Colour snapshots from the seventies and eighties. Children, adults, and elderly people—all sharing variations of the same features. The nose. The chin. The particular set of their eyes. She frowned; it seemed strange, but some of the people in the photographs looked familiar. She leaned forwards and scanned the wall from top to bottom.

And then Fern saw her. Her breath caught so hard it hurt.

A photograph from maybe thirty years ago. A young woman with silver-blonde hair caught up in a messy braid, laughing at the camera, flowers tucked behind her ear. She was standing on the bridge—Fern's bridge—and even in the photograph, even across decades, Fern could see it. The resemblance.

'That's my niece Charlotte,' Mrs Willoughby said, returning with a tea tray. 'Taken the summer she turned twenty-one. Beautiful girl. Full of life and magic and worry all mixed together.'

Fern couldn't speak.

'Charlotte used to visit every summer when she was young,' Mrs Willoughby continued, settling into the chair opposite Fern and pouring tea with steady hands. 'Loved the village. Loved the bridge especially. Said it felt like a threshold to somewhere magical.' She offered Fern a cup. 'Milk? Sugar?'

'Just milk,' Fern managed, her hands shaking as she took the cup and saucer. 'That woman in the photograph. Charlotte. What— what was her surname?'

'Willoughby, of course. Though she became Charlotte Rowan when she married.' Mrs Willoughby's eyes were sharp, knowing.

'Your mother. You have her look exactly. Same hair, same eyes, and the same way of tilting your head when you're thinking hard about something.'

Fern set down her teacup before she could drop it. 'You knew. This whole time, you knew who I was.'

'I did. I didn't tell you we were related. I thought you needed to find that out in your own time.'

'Why?' Fern's voice cracked. 'Why not just tell me?'

'Because you came here running from something, dear. Something important and frightening. And I knew—because your mother did the same thing thirty years ago—that you needed space to figure out your own heart.' Mrs Willoughby set down her cup. 'Charlotte came here the week after your father proposed. Spent ten days in this very cottage, sleeping in the spare room, crying and doubting and terrified she wasn't good enough for him.'

'Mum was scared?' Fern couldn't quite picture it. Her mother had always seemed so confident, so certain of herself and her place in the world.

'Terrified. She had the same gift you do—the flowers, the magic, the way nature responded to her. And she thought it made her strange. Unlovable. Too much for any normal person to handle.' Mrs Willoughby smiled sadly. 'Does that sound familiar, Fern?'

Tears pricked Fern's eyes. 'What happened? How did she—how did she get brave enough?'

'The village helped. And I helped, though not in the way you might think. I didn't give her answers. I just gave her space to find them herself.' Mrs Willoughby stood and walked to the mantelpiece, picking up the photograph of a young Charlotte. 'I told her what I'm going to tell you now. That magic isn't a curse or a burden. It's just another way of being real. And that love doesn't require you to be perfect or normal or anything other than yourself.'

She handed the photograph to Fern, who took it with trembling hands.

'She went home,' Mrs Willoughby continued softly. 'Called your father, said yes, married him three months later. And she was happy, Fern. Completely, wonderfully happy. She chose joy instead of fear, and she never regretted it.'

'And then she died,' Fern whispered. 'But she was always happy.

'Yes, it is very sad. But, my dear, even dying, I know she was grateful for the life she'd lived. For your father. For you. For every brave choice she'd made.' Mrs Willoughby returned to her chair. 'Before she died, she wrote to me. She made me promise something. Made me promise that if you ever came to the village—and she thought you might, someday, when you needed it—I would let you find your own courage. Not give it to you. Let you earn it.'

The sobs came then, hard and gasping. Fern pressed a hand to her mouth but couldn't stop them. 'I miss her so much,' she finally managed.

'I know, dear. I miss her too. Charlotte was my favourite niece, and even though you lived a long way away, she wrote to me often. Clever and kind and brave, once she learned how to be.' Mrs Willoughby leaned forward and took Fern's hand. 'But she's not gone. Not really. She's here in you. In your magic. In your courage, when you find it. And she would be so proud of you for coming here. For running towards something instead of running away.'

They sat in silence for a while, holding hands across the space between their chairs, connected by grief and love and the closeness of family that persisted across death and time.

Mrs Willoughby stood and walked to the window, looking out over the millstream where Fern's tent glowed softly in the fading light.

'Do you remember she brought you here once? You were three, maybe four years old.'

Fern looked up, startled. 'I was here?'

'Just for an afternoon. Charlotte wanted to show you the bridge, the millstream. You were such a solemn little thing. Watchful. You stood on the bridge and stared at the water for an hour, not saying a word, just... paying attention. Really seeing it.' Mrs Willoughby smiled at the memory. 'And there were flowers. Tiny purple violets growing up through the cracks in the stone wherever your feet had been. I knew then she'd shared her gift with you.'

'I don't remember,' Fern whispered.

'You wouldn't. You were very young. But I remember.' Mrs Willoughby returned to her chair. 'Charlotte said your magic was already stronger than hers had been at that age. More flowers, more birds following you home, more... sparkle to you.'

'It's stronger here,' Fern said suddenly. 'In the village. When I'm away—in London, at university—the flowers don't happen. Or they do, but barely. A few blooms in odd places, nothing like this.' She gestured towards the window, towards the impossible profusion of February flowers she'd been leaving everywhere. 'Here, it's like I can't control it. Like it just... pours out of me.'

'That's the village recognising your gift,' Mrs Willoughby said gently. 'And amplifying it, sharing it with those who need it. The magic here is old, dear. Older than the cottages, older than the church. It's in the stones and the water and the earth itself. And it responds to people like us—like you—who carry their own magic. It recognises kindred spirits and helps them bloom.'

'People like us?' Fern caught the phrase. 'You have it too?'

Mrs Willoughby held up her hand, palm up, and for just a moment—so brief Fern almost missed it—a single snowdrop appeared in her palm. Then it faded, like morning mist.

'I did. When I was younger. When I still needed it.' She closed her hand gently. 'But I've lived in this village for eighty-three years, and somewhere along the way, I learned to let the village itself do the work. My magic went quiet. Or perhaps I just gave it to this place, let it sink into the soil, let it help others instead of just me.'

'Does it hurt? To put it away?'

'No. It's like... growing up, in a way. You give away the things you don't need anymore, so younger people can use them.' Mrs Willoughby reached over and patted Fern's hand. 'Don't worry, dear. I'm not suggesting you give yours away. You're young yet. You need your magic. It's part of who you are, and it's beautiful. I'm just saying that the village will take what you offer—the flowers, the growth, the bloom—and give it to people who need to remember that beauty still exists. That impossible things happen. That spring always comes, even after the longest winter.'

'Like it gave that to me,' Fern said softly. 'When I arrived here scared and running.'

'Exactly like that.' Mrs. Willoughby smiled. 'The village has been waiting for you, I think. Waiting for Charlotte's daughter to come home and remember what her mother knew—

that magic isn't something to hide or fear. It's something to share. Something to celebrate. Something to trust.'

They sat in comfortable silence as full dark fell outside, and Fern thought about flowers growing in stone, about magic passed from mother to daughter, about a village that had been waiting for her long before she knew she needed it.

'Thank you,' she said finally. 'For telling me all of this. For helping me understand.'

'That's what family does,' Mrs Willoughby said. 'We help each other see clearly. We remind each other of the truth when fear makes us forget.'

'Tell me about her,' Fern said eventually. 'About when she was young. Before I knew her. I want to hear everything.'

So, Mrs Willoughby told stories.

'When Charlotte was seven,' she began,

settling deeper into her chair, 'she brought home every stray animal in the village. Cats, dogs, a hedgehog once, and even a fox cub she found in the woods. My sister—your grandmother, God rest her soul—was at her wits' end. She'd find rabbits in the garden shed, birds nesting in the kitchen cupboard. Charlotte would just look at her with those big grey-green eyes and say, "But they needed help, Mummy. They asked me".'

Fern smiled through her tears. 'Did they? Ask her?'

'In their way, I suppose. She could hear them somehow. Understand them. The same gift you have with your robin, I imagine.' Mrs Willoughby refilled their teacups. 'Then, when she was fifteen—oh, this was a sight—the vicar's daughter was getting married in June. The church garden was meant to be modest. Just a few roses, some lavender, nothing fancy.

But Charlotte walked through it the morning of the wedding, and by the time the ceremony started...' She shook her head, laughing softly. 'Roses blooming in great cascades. Wisteria that hadn't flowered in years was suddenly dripping with purple. Hollyhocks as tall as a man. The bride cried it was so beautiful. Everyone said it was a miracle. Charlotte knew better. She'd hidden in the vestry, terrified she'd be blamed.'

'Was she?'

'The vicar thanked God for blessing his daughter's marriage with such abundance. Sometimes it's easier to call things miracles than to admit magic is real.' Mrs Willoughby picked up the photograph again. 'And this. This was taken the summer she turned twenty-one. Just after your father had proposed. She stood on that bridge for hours, trying to decide if she was brave enough. She told me, "What if I'm not enough for him? What if my strangeness drives him away?" I told her what I'm telling you now—that love doesn't require you to be ordinary. It just requires you to be honest.'

'And she believed you?'

'Eventually. She went home. She said yes. She married him three months later, and I know they were happy until the day she died.' Mrs Willoughby's voice gentled. 'That's what I want you to hear, Fern. She chose bravely. She chose love. And she never, ever regretted it. I am sure your young man is as fine a man as your father is.'

With each story, something in Fern's chest loosened. Her worry evaporated like the morning mist. The fear that she was fundamentally broken. The certainty that her strangeness made her unlovable. The belief that being magical meant being alone.

Her mother had been magical, too. She

had felt the same fears. And had made a brave choice despite her fear.

And if her mother could do it—could accept her gift, could believe she deserved happiness, and say yes to love—then maybe she could too.

'Thank you,' Fern said when the stories finally ended, and the fire had burned low. 'For telling me. For letting me find my own way. For being family.'

'Always, dear girl. Always.' Mrs Willoughby squeezed her hand once more. 'Now. That fine young man who proposed. Are you going to call him?'

Fern thought about bridges and courage and her mother standing in this same cottage thirty years ago, making the same decision.

'Yes,' she said. 'Tomorrow. I'll call him tomorrow.'

'Good.' Mrs Willoughby smiled. 'The

village has done its work. Now you just have to be brave enough to trust it.'

When Fern left an hour later, she carried the photograph of her mother—a gift from Mrs Willoughby. She walked back to her tent as twilight fell, holding the image of young Charlotte against her chest like a talisman.

Her mother had been scared, too. She had run to this same village, the village where she had grown up and had learned the same lessons as she found courage.

History repeating itself, Mrs Willoughby had said. But better this time. Because Fern wasn't alone in her fear, as her mother had been. She was following a path her mother had walked before her. A path that led away from doubt and towards happiness.

And tomorrow, she would call Callum. Tomorrow, she would be brave.

But tonight, she sat in her tent and

looked at the photograph of her mother on the bridge, smiling and hopeful and full of magic, and felt less alone than she had in weeks.

'I'll make you proud,' she whispered to the image. 'I promise, Mum. I'll be brave.'

And somewhere in the space between earth and whatever came after, perhaps Charlotte Rowan smiled and whispered back: 'You already are, my darling Fern. You already are.'

Chapter Five

The Celebration

The Old Swan at seven o'clock on a February evening was exactly what a village pub should be—warm, welcoming, and humming with gentle conversation. Dimity pushed open the heavy wooden door, Vivian's hand in hers, and was immediately enveloped by the scent of woodsmoke, ale, and something delicious cooking in the kitchen.

Low oak beams crossed the ceiling, dark with age and smoke, forcing taller patrons to duck as they moved between the bar and the scattered tables. Horse brasses gleamed on the walls beside old hunting prints, and a fire crackled in an enormous stone fireplace that dominated the far wall. The flagstone floor was worn smooth by generations of feet, and the pub had the comfortable, lived-in feel that came from three hundred years of serving pints.

'Welcome!' Alf Cooper's voice boomed from behind the bar. He was a bear of a man, easily six foot four, with a grey beard that would have done a Viking proud, and eyes that crinkled with perpetual good humour. 'Heard you had news worth celebrating. Netflix, is it? Means I'll get to watch one of your books now, Dimity.'

'You can't watch books, Alf,' Dimity said, smiling as she approached the bar. 'They're making them into a series. A show.'

'Same difference.' Alf waved a massive hand dismissively. 'Moving pictures with a story. I'll watch it. Might even understand it, if you're lucky.' He leaned on the bar, his expression turning conspiratorial. 'Now then. What happened when the Netflix executive walked into a pub?'

Vivian groaned. 'Oh no, here we go.'

'He ordered a series!' Alf slapped the bar, delighted with himself. 'Get it? A series! Because they make series, but also you can order drinks in a series, like rounds—'

'We get it, Alf,' Dimity laughed. 'It's terrible.'

'All my best jokes are terrible. That's what makes them memorable.' He grabbed a cloth and began wiping down the already-spotless bar. 'Are Hugh and Joanna coming?'

'Should be here any minute,' Vivian said. 'We're celebrating properly tonight. Now that Dimity's finally made it big.'

'She was already big. Now she's just expensive.' Alf winked. 'What can I get you while you're waiting? First round's on the house. Can't have our local celebrity paying for drinks on her big night.'

'Alf, you don't have to—'

'I absolutely do. This village takes care of its own, and you're one of ours now. Permanent resident and everything.' He pulled two glasses from beneath the bar. 'What'll it be?'

The door opened again, bringing in a gust of cold air and Hugh and Joanna. Hugh had his arm around Joanna's waist, guiding her through the door with the careful gentleness of new love. She looked lovely tonight, Dimity thought—wearing a deep blue jumper that brought out her eyes, her hair loose around her shoulders for once instead of tied back.

'You're here finally!' Alf bellowed. 'Right, that's it. Everyone's drinking champagne tonight. I've got a bottle in the back I've been saving for something special.'

'Alf, we can't let you—' Hugh started. 'We brought—'

'You can and you will. This young lady

here—' he pointed at Dimity, '—just put our village on the map. When those Netflix people come scouting locations, they'll see The Old Swan in all its glory, and I'll be serving pints to film stars before you know it.' He disappeared through a door behind the bar, still talking. 'I'll have George Clooney sitting right where you're standing, mark my words!'

'Does he know George Clooney's not in the Netflix deal?' Joanna asked quietly.

'Best not to tell him,' Vivian said. 'He's having too much fun.'

They settled at a table near the fire—a round oak table that had probably been in the pub since it opened, its surface scarred with centuries of use and initials carved by bored customers. The warmth from the fireplace was immediate and glorious, and Dimity relaxed properly for the first time since Vivian had insisted they tell people about the Netflix deal.

Alf returned with champagne and four glasses, popping the cork with theatrical flair that made an elderly couple at the next table jump. 'Right then. To Dimity March—Lower Thistlewick's answer to Agatha Christie, Jane Austen, Enid Blyton, and whoever writes those dragon books the youngsters like!'

'George R.R. Martin,' Hugh supplied.

'Him too. To Dimity!' Alf poured champagne with surprising elegance for such large hands.

They toasted, the champagne cold and fizzing, and Alf retreated to the bar with a satisfied nod.

'He's really very sweet,' Joanna said, watching him serve another customer with the same enthusiasm he'd shown them. 'I wasn't sure about the village pub when I first arrived. Thought they'd be all old men being suspicious of newcomers. Then again, I was scared of the whole village.' Her chuckle was low and musical.

'Alf's suspicious of everyone,' Hugh said. 'But only until he's decided you're all right. Then you're family.' He raised his glass again. 'To Dimity. Properly this time. You've worked so hard for this. You deserve every bit of success coming your way.'

'Hear, hear,' Vivian said softly, squeezing Dimity's hand under the table.

'I still can't quite believe it,' Dimity admitted. 'A year ago, I was writing, wondering if I was wasting my time. Then I found a beautiful agent, I was published, and now this.'

'Look how far you've come. Four months ago, you couldn't even see.'

Joanna's expression shifted, became more attentive. 'You couldn't see?'

'Long story,' Dimity said.

'We have all evening,' Hugh said,

standing. 'But first, I'm getting proper drinks. Champagne's lovely, but I want a pint. Joanna?'

'White wine, please.'

'Vivian?'

'Same. A pint, please.'

'Dimity?'

'Cider, if Alf has any decent stuff.'

The men headed to the bar, leaving Dimity and Joanna alone at the table. The fire crackled beside them, and an aroma of garlic wafted from the kitchen.

'You really couldn't see?' Joanna asked quietly. 'What happened?'

Dimity hesitated, then thought: why not? Joanna had her own story—Hugh had mentioned it briefly, the years of caring for dying parents, the exhaustion and grief. They'd both been broken in different ways.

'I had an accident in London,' Dimity said. 'In November. I was on my way to meet my publisher, got a text from my agent about the Netflix interest—this was the first time they approached, before the actual deal—and I got so excited I wasn't watching where I was going. Fell on some stone steps outside the publishing house. Hit my head.'

'God.' Joanna's hand went to her mouth.

'Traumatic brain injury. Not severe enough to kill me, but severe enough to damage my optic nerves.' Dimity could talk about it now without the old panic rising. Time and healing had helped. 'I woke up in hospital completely blind. The doctors said it might be temporary, might be permanent. No way to know.'

'That's terrifying.'

'It was. The blindness itself, yes, but also—I'm a writer. I write on a computer. I type fast, I edit as I go, I see the words on the screen.' Dimity shook her head at the memory.

'I thought my career was over. All the Netflix interest, the book deals, everything I'd worked for—gone because I wasn't watching where I put my feet.'

Joanna reached across the table and took Dimity's hand. The gesture was spontaneous, warm, and Dimity felt tears prick her eyes.

'But you can see now,' Joanna said.

'It came back. Slowly, over weeks. Blurry at first, then clearer. The doctors said traumatic brain injuries were unpredictable.' Dimity smiled. 'But I like to believe it was the cottage.'

'Pippin's Nook?'

'Mmm. My great-aunt Bea left it to me when she died—and that's where I wrote my first book before I went travelling. This is where I met Vivian. My agent hired a female editor because some of my scenes are well...' She smiled and looked over at the bar where

Vivian was standing beside Hugh. 'Instead of a Vivienne as we expected, a male Vivan arrived, and we worked together really well.'

'And you fell in love,' Joanna said softly. 'I thought you had been together a long time.'

'As well as falling in love, the cottage—' Dimity paused, trying to find words for something that sounded crazy when spoken aloud. 'The cottage helped me. The village helped me. I know that sounds strange.'

'It doesn't,' Joanna said firmly. 'I know exactly what you are saying. Hawthorn Cottage helped me too. I arrived here broken, grieving, with no money and no hope. And the cottage— it kept me warm when I had no idea how to work the heating. It gave me space to breathe. It made me believe I could be happy again.' She looked at Dimity with sudden intensity. 'You don't think I'm crazy for believing that?'

'Not even slightly. Everyone in this village believes the cottages are magic. Why shouldn't we? We're both permanent residents now. I truly appreciate your friendship, Joanna.'

They sat in comfortable silence, the fire warm beside them. Two women separated by almost thirty years in age, but connected by healing and the strange magic of a Cotswold village that knew exactly what its residents needed.

'What was the hardest part?' Joanna asked eventually. 'Of losing your sight?'

'The loss of independence,' Dimity said immediately. 'I've always been self-sufficient. After I left Australia, I lived alone and worked alone, managing my own life. Suddenly, I needed to learn everything again. Getting dressed, making tea, walking to the bathroom.' She glanced across to where Vivian stood at the bar with Hugh, laughing at something Alf had said. 'I wouldn't let Vivian help with anything except my book. He was amazing. Patient, kind, and never once made me feel like a burden.' Dimity's voice went soft. 'That's what the blindness gave me, oddly. Proof that falling in love doesn't need perfect circumstances. That someone can see you at your absolute worst and still choose to stay.'

'That's so beautiful.' Joanna's eyes were bright with unshed tears. 'I spent ten years caring for my parents. Watching them fade, cleaning up after them, feeding them, bathing them. And I never once thought of it as a burden. I loved them. That's what you do for people you love.'

Dimity squeezed Joanna's hand. 'How are things with Hugh? You two seem happy.'

Joanna's face transformed, joy breaking through like sunlight. 'We are. It's strange—I came here thinking I'd be alone forever. Fifty-one years old, parents dead, divorced, broke, living in a cottage I'd inherited from a distant cousin. Not exactly the beginning of a romance novel.'

'The best ones always start with the heroine at her lowest point,' Dimity said. 'Trust me, I write them. The happy ending is sweeter when you've earned it through suffering.'

'Is that what we're doing? Earning our happy endings?'

'I think we already have them.' Dimity looked around the pub—at the warm firelight, the oak beams, the friendly faces. At Vivian and Hugh returning with drinks, both smiling, easy in each other's company. 'This is it. This moment, right here. This is the happy ending.'

The men arrived back at the table laden with glasses—Hugh balancing a tray, Vivian catching the cider before it could tip. 'What are we celebrating now?' Hugh asked, seeing the women still holding hands across the table. 'You two look very serious.'

'Friendship,' Joanna said simply.

'The magic kind,' Dimity added.

'Ah. The best kind.' Vivian distributed drinks, then raised his pint glass. 'To friendship. To magic. To villages that know what we need before we do.'

'To The Old Swan,' Hugh added. 'And to Alf's terrible jokes.'

'I heard that!' Alf called from the bar. 'And my jokes are brilliant. Here's another one for you—why did the author go to the pub?'

'Why?' they chorused dutifully.

'Because she needed some character development!' Alf slapped the bar again, roaring with laughter at his own joke.

'That's actually not bad,' Dimity admitted.

'Don't encourage him,' an old man at the

bar said, but he was smiling.

They ordered food—shepherd's pie all round, with extra gravy—and the conversation continued.

'So, Emma's Romans project,' Joanna said, turning to Hugh with a smile. 'How's that coming along?'

Hugh groaned. 'There's glitter everywhere. Everywhere. I found some in my coffee this morning. I have no idea how it got there.'

'What's she making?' Dimity asked.

'A model of the Colosseum. Out of papier-mâché. Which apparently requires industrial quantities of glue, paint, and—'

'Glitter,' Vivian finished, grinning. 'Obviously. What's a gladiatorial arena without sparkle?'

'She insisted the sand needed to shimmer,' Hugh said. 'Because apparently

Roman sand was magical. I tried to explain that it wasn't historically accurate, but she gave me a look that said I was being boring.'

'She's not wrong,' Joanna said, laughing. 'You were being boring.'

'Thank you for that.' But Hugh was smiling. 'I've been helping her with the essay part. Turns out I know more about Julius Caesar than I thought.'

'All those years selling history books are finally paying off,' Dimity said. When Alf brought out the shepherd's pies—massive portions, crusted with golden potato and fragrant with herbs—they tucked in with the enthusiasm of people who'd been drinking on empty stomachs.

'Joanna,' Vivian said after a few mouthfuls, 'Hugh mentioned you're planting a vegetable garden? At Hawthorn Cottage?'

'Trying to. For spring.' Joanna looked

slightly embarrassed. 'I've never gardened before. I lived in London my whole life until last year. But the cottage has this beautiful space out back, and it seems a shame to waste it.'

'What are you thinking of growing?' Dimity asked.

'Tomatoes, definitely. Courgettes. Maybe some herbs—basil, thyme, rosemary. Whatever's foolproof for beginners.' Joanna laughed. 'Though I'm not sure anything's foolproof when I'm involved. I killed a cactus once.'

'How does someone kill a cactus?' Hugh asked, delighted.

'Overwatering. I felt sorry for it.' Joanna shrugged. 'I'm very nurturing. Fatally so, apparently.'

'You'll do fine with a vegetable garden,' Dimity assured her. 'Tomatoes are nearly impossible to kill. And herbs actively want to take over the world. Just plant them and stand back.'

'I could help, if you'd like,' Vivian offered. 'My grandparents had a farm in Devon. My grandfather had a kitchen garden that could feed half the village. I used to love pulling the carrots and eating them when I visited as a child. He taught me a lot about soil and sun, too.'

'Really?' Joanna's face lit up. 'That would be amazing. I was going to just buy gardening books and hope for the best.'

'Books help,' Vivian said. 'But mostly you just need to pay attention to the plants. They'll tell you what they need if you listen.'

'You're starting to sound like Iris Willoughby,' Hugh observed.

'Farmers are mystical,' Vivian said seriously. 'They just hide it behind practical language. It's all magic, just dressed up as common sense.'

'Like the village,' Dimity said softly.

'Exactly like the village,' Hugh agreed. 'Everything here is magic dressed up as ordinary life. Or maybe it's the other way around—ordinary life revealing the magic that was always there.'

'Speaking of which,' Dimity leaned forward conspiratorially, 'has anyone else noticed the flowers following Fern around? The fairy girl?'

'Hard to miss,' Hugh said. 'Emma's convinced they're proof of magic. I'm inclined to agree.'

'I saw violets blooming where she walked,' Joanna said. 'In February. That's not normal, is it?'

'Nothing about this village is normal,' Vivian pointed out. 'That's why we love it.'

'True.' Dimity raised her glass. 'To the village. And to new friends who don't think we're completely mad for believing in impossible things.'

'To the village,' they chorused, glasses clinking together over the shepherd's pie.

'And to Emma's glitter,' Joanna added. 'May it sparkle forever in inappropriate places.'

Hugh groaned, but he was laughing. 'Don't encourage her.'

And through it all, warmth settled in Dimity's chest. Contentment. Belonging. The joy of being exactly where she was meant to be, surrounded by people who understood you.

Alf came to clear the plates when they finished 'Can I say something?' he asked, suddenly serious.

'Of course,' Hugh said.

'This village—it's special. Always has been. People come here when they're broken, when they need something they can't find anywhere else. And the village—' He gestured vaguely at the walls, the beams, the fire. 'It fixes them. I don't know how, don't ask me to explain it. But I've seen it happen over and over. People arrive lost, and leave found.'

'Very philosophical for a publican,' Hugh teased gently.

'There's more to me than pulling pints,' Alf said with dignity. 'Point is, you four— you're all part of that now. Part of the village's magic. And I'm glad you're here. All of you.' He nodded once, firmly, then returned to the bar before anyone could respond.

'He's right, you know,' Hugh said quietly. 'About the village. I came here five years ago with a grieving daughter and a broken heart. And look at us now.'

'I came here blind and terrified,' Dimity said. 'And now I can see again. Literally and metaphorically.'

'I came here with nothing,' Joanna said. 'And found everything.'

'I came here and found my love.' Vivian smiled and raised his glass. 'To Lower Thistlewick. May it always know exactly what we need.'

They touched glasses, the sound bright and clear in the warm pub, and outside, February settled over the village with frost and starlight.

Just when they thought they couldn't eat another bite, Alf appeared at their table with a gleam in his eye.

'Right then,' he announced. 'Who's having pudding?'

A chorus of groans greeted this suggestion.

'Alf, I can't move,' Dimity protested.

'Can't leave The Old Swan without

trying the sticky toffee pudding. House specialty. My gran's recipe.' Alf crossed his arms. 'You'd be insulting her memory if you refused.'

'That's emotional blackmail,' Hugh said.

'It's called good business.' Alf grinned. 'Four sticky toffee puddings, or would anyone prefer the apple crumble? Made this morning. Bramley apples from Mrs Pemberton's orchard.'

'Apple crumble,' Joanna said, caving immediately. 'With custard.'

'That's the spirit.' Alf looked at the others expectantly.

'Okay,' Vivian said. 'Sticky toffee pudding.'

'Make that two,' Hugh added.

'Three,' Dimity sighed. 'But if I can't fit through the door afterwards, you're carrying me home.'

'Done.' Alf disappeared back toward the kitchen, whistling.

The puddings arrived ten minutes later—the sticky toffee swimming in toffee sauce, the crumble topped with a mountain of steaming custard. They were, as Alf had promised, perfect.

'Your gran knew what she was doing,' Vivian said, scraping his bowl clean.

'She usually did,' Alf called from the bar. 'Took no nonsense and made the best puddings in three counties. I miss her every day.'

They stayed until closing time, laughing and talking and making plans—Vivian promising to help Joanna with her garden in spring, Hugh inviting everyone to Emma's school play in March, Dimity mentioning a reading she was planning at the bookshop. When they finally emerged into the cold night, slightly tipsy and certainly overfed, the village green was silver with frost under a clear sky brilliant with stars.

'That was perfect,' Joanna said, leaning into Hugh as they walked. 'Absolutely perfect.'

'Alf's jokes notwithstanding,' Hugh agreed.

'Especially Alf's jokes,' Dimity corrected. 'They were awful. Wonderfully, terribly awful.'

'Character development,' Vivian snorted. 'I'm going to be laughing about that for days.'

They paused at the bridge—the central meeting point, the heart of the village—and stood looking at the cottages clustered around the green. Lights glowed in windows. Smoke rose from chimneys. Everything was quiet and still and magical.

'You know what Mrs Willoughby said

the other day?' Dimity said, looking over at Fern's tent bathed in a golden glow. 'About more happy developments coming to the village?'

'She was right, wasn't she?' Joanna said softly. 'That girl—Fern—she's part of it.'

'She's running from something,' Hugh said quietly. 'You can see it in how she moves. Like she's not quite sure she's allowed to stay.'

'That's what bridges do,' Vivian said, leaning against the stone wall. 'They're decision points. Eventually, you have to choose—go forward or go back. But you can't stay on a bridge forever.'

'Deep thoughts from a man who's had three pints,' Dimity teased, slipping her hand into his.

'Three pints and sticky toffee pudding,' Vivian corrected. 'That's when I'm at my most philosophical.'

'She'll choose forward,' Dimity said with a smile. 'The village won't let her keep running. It never does.'

They stood together in comfortable silence, four people who'd all made their own crossings—toward love, toward healing, toward home.

'I wonder what she's running from,' Joanna murmured.

'Love, probably,' Vivian said. 'It's usually love. The thing that scares us most is the thing we want most.'

Dimity squeezed his hand, and they said their goodnights—Dimity and Vivian to Pippin's Nook, Hugh towards home and Emma, Joanna to Hawthorn Cottage.

And in her tent on the village green, Fern lay awake thinking about a boy she'd left behind and wondering if courage was something you found or something you'd always had, just buried under fear.

Tomorrow, she would read to the children again. Tomorrow, the village would work on her a little more.

Tomorrow, she would take one small step closer to going home.

Chapter Six

Stories by the Water

The idea came from Emma, naturally.

'Why read inside when we could read by the bridge?' she'd asked Fern on Saturday morning, appearing at the tent just after dawn with a thermos of hot chocolate from her grandmother. 'The bridge is the best place in the village. You said so yourself.'

Fern had said no such thing, but looking at Emma's hopeful face, she found herself nodding. 'You're absolutely right. The bridge is perfect.'

By three o'clock that afternoon, half the village had turned out.

Children lined both banks of the millstream, sitting on the winter grass with blankets and cushions their mothers had packed.

Parents stood in clusters behind them, ostensibly supervising but really just as curious as their offspring. Fern could see Hugh and Joanna near the bookshop side, Margaret from The Cosy Cup with a basket of biscuits, and even grumpy Tom from the pub looking interested despite himself.

Fern sat on the bridge wall, exactly where Emma had first found her, with her legs dangling over the water and a book in her lap. The robin perched on the stone beside her, and the millstream flowed beneath, constant and musical.

'This is perfect,' Emma breathed, sitting cross-legged at Fern's feet on the bridge itself. 'You look like a proper fairy now. Like you belong here.'

'I'm just a girl with a book,' Fern said, but her voice was soft.

'You're a fairy,' Emma insisted.

'Everyone knows it.'

Fern looked out at the assembled crowd—at least twenty children, and nearly as many adults pretending they weren't there for the story. The afternoon light caught the water, making it sparkle. Snowdrops bloomed impossibly along both banks, even though they shouldn't be flowering yet. The air smelled of cold earth and coming spring.

She thought about Callum. About how he'd asked her to marry him, his face so full of hope and terror. About how she'd said she needed to think, needed time, needed space. About how she'd packed a bag that night and disappeared into the countryside because she was a coward who ran from the things that mattered most.

'Right then,' she said, opening the book. Her voice carried perfectly over the water, amplified by something that might have been acoustics or might have been the village's particular magic. 'Has anyone here heard the story of the Water Babies?'

A few hands went up, tentative.

'Well, you haven't heard it the way I tell it.' Fern smiled at them, at all these children who believed in magic simply because they were too young to know better. 'This is a story about a boy named Tom, who was dirty and unloved and thought he'd always be small and worthless. But then he fell into a stream—not unlike this one—and something magical happened.'

She began to read, and the millstream seemed to quiet beneath her, as if it too wanted to listen.

Fern had always been good at reading aloud. Her mother had taught her that stories weren't just words on a page—they were living things, breathing things, creatures that needed voice and belief to come fully alive. So, when she read about Tom falling into the water, she let her voice ripple and flow. When she read about the water babies, she made them sound like laughter, bubbles, and joy.

And the strangest thing happened.

The millstream began to glow.

Just faintly, just at the edges, but Emma saw it. Hugh saw it. Even Tom from the pub, who'd never believed in anything he couldn't drink from a glass, saw it and blinked hard, as if trying to clear his vision.

'She's doing it,' a child whispered. 'She's making the magic real.'

But Fern wasn't doing anything except reading a story she loved to people who wanted to believe in it. If the water glowed, if the air shimmered, if snowdrops multiplied along the banks while she spoke—well. That was the village's doing, not hers.

Or perhaps it was both.

She read for an hour, until the light began to fail and mothers started collecting children for supper. When she finally closed the book, the spell broke gently, leaving only the sound of the millstream and the rustle of people gathering belongings.

'Tomorrow?' Emma asked, already knowing the answer.

'Tomorrow,' Fern agreed. 'Same place, same time.'

The children dispersed reluctantly, looking back over their shoulders as if worried Fern might vanish like morning mist. Parents thanked her warmly, appreciating that their children had been entertained for an hour.

As they had.

Hugh caught Fern's eye across the green and nodded with a smile.

Only Dimity remained, standing on the

far bank with her hands in her coat pockets, watching Fern with an expression that was gentle and knowing all at once.

'That was lovely,' she said, crossing the bridge to stand beside Fern. 'You have a gift.'

'I just like stories.' Fern slid off the bridge wall, suddenly aware of how cold the stone had become beneath her. Funny how she never felt it while she was reading.

'It's more than that.' Dimity fell into step beside Fern as they walked along the millstream path, away from the cottages, toward the meadow beyond. 'You make people believe things are possible. That's not a small magic.'

'I only read stories. You have the real talent, Dimity.' Fern's voice went shy again. 'You create the stories, the characters, their lives, the worlds they live in. I loved Lord Ashton from your first book—the way you created the tension between him and Elara.'

'Thank you.' Dimity looked pleased. 'He was my favourite to write. Hiding such desperate longing.'

'You could see it,' Fern said. 'It's brilliant writing.'

'But you brought *The Water Babies* to life today.' Dimity's tone was gentle but firm. 'You made the millstream glow. Made people believe in transformation and becoming clean and new. That's not a small thing, Fern. Don't dismiss your gift just because it's different from mine.'

'I'm not magical.' The words came out sharper than Fern intended. 'I'm just a girl who's camping because she's too much of a coward to face real life.'

'Ah.' Dimity's voice was warm with understanding. 'Running from something, are we?'

Fern stopped walking. Around them, the

February meadow was brown and dormant, waiting for spring. But where her feet had touched the path, small purple violets had appeared. She looked down at them, at this evidence of something she couldn't control, couldn't explain, and tears pricked her eyes.

'Someone asked me to marry him,' she said to the violets. 'And instead of saying yes or no, I ran away to live in a tent and read stories to children. What kind of person does that?'

'The kind who's frightened.' Dimity's hand was gentle on Fern's shoulder. 'The kind who doesn't believe she deserves happiness. The kind who thinks that if she stays still too long, all the good things might disappear. When I met Vivian, I learned that running doesn't make you safe. It just makes you lonely.'

They walked in silence for a while, following the millstream as it wound through the meadow. Flowers continued to bloom in

Fern's wake—not just violets now, but primroses and crocuses, as if her distress was calling spring early.

'Do you love him?' Dimity asked eventually. 'This man who proposed?'

'Yes.' The word came out broken. 'So much it terrifies me.'

'Why?'

'Because what if I'm not enough? What if he sees who I really am and regrets it? What if I'm just—' Fern gestured helplessly at herself, at the flowers, at the whole impossible situation. 'What if I'm too strange, too odd, too much of a fairy tale and not enough of a real person?'

'Fern.' Dimity stopped walking and turned to face her properly. 'Look at what you've done in three days. You've made children believe in magic. You've brought the village together. You've left flowers blooming in February. That's not too much. That's exactly enough.'

'But what if—'

'What if he loves you because you're strange and odd and magical? What if those aren't flaws but gifts? What if running away is the only real mistake you could make?'

Fern looked back toward the village. From here, she could see the bridge, the cottages clustered around the green, and smoke rising from chimneys into the winter sky. It looked like an illustration from a children's book. A place where magic was possible. Where happy endings happened.

'I don't know if I have the courage go back,' she said quietly. 'I have written to him since I've been here.'

Dimity's voice was firm but kind. 'You have to trust that love is braver than fear.'

'What if he says it is too late?'

'Then at least you tried. At least you crossed the bridge instead of standing on it forever, too scared to move either direction.'

Fern looked down at the path. Flowers bloomed thick now, a carpet of spring colours in the winter grass. The millstream sang beside them, constant and sure, flowing forward because that was what water did. It didn't stop. It didn't run backwards. It just kept going, finding its way around obstacles, wearing down rocks, eventually reaching the sea.

'I should go back,' Fern said, testing the words.

'You should.' Dimity squeezed her shoulder once more, then stepped back. 'But not yet, I think. First, you should finish your week here. Let the village work on you a bit more. Let yourself believe that you're someone worth loving.'

'I'm not sure a week is long enough for

that.'

'Then stay longer. Stay until you're sure.' Dimity smiled. 'Your tent's not going anywhere. And neither are we.'

They walked back to the village together as twilight fell. When they reached the bridge, Fern stopped and looked down at the millstream, at its dark water reflecting the first stars.

'Thank you,' she said.

'We've all run from something.' Dimity's expression was gentle. 'The trick is learning when to stop running and turn around. When to trust that the thing chasing you might actually be the thing you need most.'

After Dimity left, Fern stood on the bridge for a long time, watching the water flow beneath her feet. The robin appeared from somewhere and settled on her shoulder, warm despite the cold.

'What do you think?' she asked it. 'Should I go home now?'

The robin chirped, which could have meant anything.

'Helpful,' Fern muttered. But she was smiling.

She returned to her tent as full dark fell and found a basket waiting outside. Inside was a thermos of soup, fresh bread wrapped in a tea towel, and a note in neat handwriting: *Thought you might be cold. The soup is vegetable. The bread is still warm. Welcome to our village, dear. You belong here as long as you need to. - Aunt Iris Willoughby*

Fern crawled into her tent, drank the soup, and fell asleep thinking about bridges and millstreams and the difference between running from something and running toward it.

Outside, where she'd walked with

Dimity, the meadow path bloomed with flowers that would remain until spring came properly. A gift from a girl who didn't believe in her own magic.

Chapter Seven

Frost and Flowers

Fern woke on Sunday morning to discover frost on her tent.

Not just a light dusting, but a proper February frost, the kind that made grass crunch underfoot and turned the millstream's edges to lace. She crawled out of her sleeping bag, pulled on her cardigan, and unzipped the tent to find the entire village transformed into a winter wonderland.

Everything was white. Everything except the path she'd walked yesterday with Dimity, which still blazed with colour—purple violets, yellow primroses, white snowdrops, even early crocuses in lavender and gold.

'Oh,' Fern breathed. 'Oh dear.'

Because there was no hiding this. No

pretending the flowers were a coincidence or a trick of the light. The contrast was too stark, too obvious. She might as well have painted **I AM ACTUALLY MAGIC** across the village green in neon letters.

She was still staring at the evidence of her being different when Emma appeared, wearing a puffer coat and wellies, her breath making clouds in the cold air.

'Fern!' Emma's shout carried across the green. 'Fern! Come look at what you did!'

'I didn't do anything,' Fern said weakly.

'You made a flower path! Come see!' Emma grabbed Fern's hand—she'd ventured out barefoot again, because apparently, cold genuinely didn't bother her feet—and dragged her toward the millstream.

The path wasn't just blooming. It was glowing.

Faint, like the millstream had glowed

during yesterday's reading, but definitely there. A soft golden light that made the frost sparkle and the flowers look like something from a medieval illumination. People were already gathering to look, coming out of cottages in dressing gowns and coats, pointing and exclaiming.

'It's a miracle,' Mrs Pemberton announced to anyone who'd listen.

'It's that girl,' Tom from the pub said, but not unkindly. 'The fairy one.'

'I'm not a fairy,' Fern tried to say, but Emma shushed her.

'Yes, you are. Everyone knows. And look—you made something beautiful. Why are you worried?'

Why indeed? Fern looked at the path, at the spring flowers blooming in February frost, and tried to articulate the fear that had lived in her chest for as long as she could remember.

That being different meant being alone. That magic was just another word for strange. That if people saw what she really was, they'd stop seeing her as a person and start seeing her as a thing.

But these people weren't looking at her with fear or suspicion. They were looking at the flowers with delight. With wonder. With the sort of joy that came from witnessing something impossible and choosing to be happy about it rather than judging her.

'Come on,' Emma said, tugging her hand. 'Let's walk the whole path. I want to see where it goes.'

They walked together, Emma pointing out the different flowers, Fern quiet and overwhelmed. The path led from the village green, along the millstream, into the meadow, then curved back toward the cottages, ending at the bridge where Fern had first sat reading.

A perfect circle. Or perhaps more accurately, a bridge between two places: the village and the wild, the ordinary and the magical, the life Fern was running from and the life she could choose instead.

'It's telling a story,' Emma said suddenly.

'What?'

'The path. It's telling a story. Look.' Emma gestured at the beginning, near Fern's tent. 'It starts small and scared—just little violets. Then it gets braver—primroses and crocuses. Then in the meadow, it gets wild and happy—all the colours together. And then it comes home to the bridge, where it started. It's your story, Fern. It's about running away and coming back.'

Fern stared at the twelve-year-old who'd somehow understood what she herself had only just begun to understand.

'How did you get so wise?' she managed.

'My mum taught me. She used to say that magic tells the truth even when people can't.' Emma's expression went distant for a moment, sad, then cleared. 'I remember her saying that the cottages here helped people by showing them what was true. Maybe the flowers are doing the same for you.'

Before Fern could respond, Hugh appeared, crossing the bridge toward them. He was carrying a proper coat and held it out to her.

'Thought you might need this, Fern. It's getting colder, and I know you claim not to feel it, but...' He trailed off, looking at the flowers, at the frost, at his daughter standing hand-in-hand with a girl who left spring in her footsteps. 'Joanna sent it. It was hers, but she has others.'

'That's very kind.' Fern took the jacket,

surprised by how heavy it was, how solid. Real. A real coat for a real person, not a fairy or a story, but a girl who needed warmth. 'Thank her for me?'

'Tell her yourself. She wants you to come to Sunday lunch. At Hawthorn Cottage. One o'clock, if you're free.'

'I don't want to impose—'

'She wants to talk about books.' Hugh's smile was gentle. 'And I think she wants to make sure you're eating properly. She worries.'

'Everyone here worries,' Fern said, but she was smiling too.

'It's what our village does. We look after each other.' Hugh glanced at Emma. 'Come on, Em. Let's leave Fern to her morning. We've got stock to catalogue this morning.'

'But the flowers—'

'Will still be there this afternoon. And you have maths homework that you've had for three days, which is due on Monday if I remember correctly.'

Emma groaned but allowed herself to be led away, waving dramatically at Fern over her shoulder. Hugh paused at the bridge, looked back at the flower path, and shook his head.

Fern stood alone in the frost and flowers and tried to remember how to breathe normally.

This wasn't what was supposed to happen. She'd come here to hide, to think, to avoid making decisions. Instead, the village was holding up a mirror and making her look at herself. Making her see that magic wasn't something to fear or suppress—it was just part of who she was. Like Emma's wisdom, Hugh's kindness, or the village's inexplicable ability to help people find what they needed.

She thought about Callum. About how he'd never asked her to be less than she was. How he'd loved the strangeness in her, had encouraged it, had laughed with delight when flowers appeared in unexpected places or birds followed her home.

She missed him desperately. Missed talking to him about everything and nothing. Missed his voice—that deep, warm rumble that made her feel safe. Missed looking into his brown eyes and seeing love there, uncomplicated and certain, even when she couldn't understand why he loved her. Missed the way he'd tuck her hair behind her ear when she was reading, or bring her tea without being asked, or text her ridiculous jokes in the middle of his workday just to make her smile.

She knew she loved him. Had always known, really, from the first month they'd been together. Knew she couldn't leave him, wouldn't be able to survive without him in her life. But she had to get over this—this bone-deep certainty that she was too strange, too magical, too much. That eventually he'd wake up and see what she saw: a girl who grew flowers by accident and talked to birds and couldn't fit into the normal world no matter how hard she tried.

How she'd been the one who thought it was too much, too odd, too likely to drive him away eventually.

What if Emma was right? What if the flowers were telling her story? Running scared, growing wild, coming home to the bridge—to the crossing point, the decision point, the place where you either moved forward or stayed frozen forever?

'Not yet,' she told the flowers, told herself, told the universe that seemed determined to push her toward courage. 'I'm not ready yet.'

But even as she said it, she knew it was a lie. She was as ready as she'd ever be. She was just frightened.

And fear, she was learning, wasn't a good reason to refuse happiness.

***

At one o'clock, Fern knocked on the door of Hawthorn Cottage.

Joanna answered immediately, as if she'd been waiting, and ushered Fern into warmth and light and the smell of something delicious baking.

'I made soup,' Joanna said. 'And bread. I hope you're hungry.'

'Starving.' It was true. Fern had been too unsettled to eat breakfast, and the morning's emotional revelations had left her hollow.

They ate at a small table by the window, overlooking the garden. Outside, Hawthorn Cottage's grounds showed the same winter dormancy as everywhere else, but Fern could feel the potential in them. The sleeping roses, the hibernating herbs, the bulbs waiting underground for the signal to grow.

'You understand plants,' Joanna said, watching Fern's gaze drift across the garden.

'I've always been good with them. They just... respond to me.'

'Like the flowers on the path.' Joanna's voice was matter-of-fact, not wondering or suspicious, just accepting. 'Hugh told me. The whole village is talking about it.'

'I'm sorry—'

'Don't be.' Joanna leaned forward, earnest. 'Fern, this village is magic. We all know it. The cottages help people. Things bloom at impossible times. Lost things get found. People come here broken and leave whole. Your flowers are just another piece of that. They're not strange—they're perfect.'

Fern felt something tight in her chest loosen slightly. 'You really believe that?'

'I know it.' Joanna smiled. 'I came here six months ago to grieve after I'd spent a long time caring for my parents, and when they were gone, I didn't know who I was anymore. I thought I was just a caregiver. Just someone who existed to serve others. And this cottage—' She gestured at the walls around them. 'It taught me I was allowed to have my own life. My own joy. My own love.'

'Hugh,' Fern said quietly.

'Hugh.' Joanna's expression went soft. 'And Emma. And this whole impossible village. But it started with the cottage making me see I deserved happiness. That spending your life caring for others doesn't mean you're not allowed to care for yourself too.'

Fern looked down at her soup, at the steam rising from it, at the simple kindness of someone making sure she was fed and warm.

'Someone asked me to marry him,' she

said, the words spilling out before she could stop them. 'And I ran away because I was terrified I'd mess it up. That I'd be too much or not enough or both at once. That he'd realise he'd made a mistake and I'd already be too in love to recover.'

'Do you love him?'

'More than anything.'

'And does he know about—' Joanna gestured vaguely at Fern, at the magic she carried.

'Yes. He's never minded. He thinks it's wonderful.' Fern's voice broke. 'He thinks I'm wonderful. And I don't understand why.'

'Because you are.' Joanna reached across the table and took Fern's hand. 'You're brave and kind, and you make children believe in magic. You read stories as though they matter. You leave flowers everywhere you go. Why wouldn't he love you?'

'Because I ran away instead of saying yes.'

'Then talk to him. Tell him you were frightened.' Joanna squeezed Fern's hand.

Fern thought about bridges. About crossing points. About the moment when you stepped off solid ground and trusted that there was something firm on the other side.

'I don't have my phone,' she admitted. 'I left it at my flat. I thought if I brought it, I'd be tempted to check it. To see if he'd called. To torture myself.'

'Use mine.' Joanna was already pulling her mobile from her pocket. 'Call him now. Before you lose your nerve.'

'Now?' Fern's voice went up an octave. 'But—'

'Now. I'll give you privacy. I need to check the garden anyway.' Joanna pressed the phone into Fern's hand, then stood and pulled on a coat. 'Take as long as you need. I'll be outside.'

And then she was gone, and Fern was alone in Hawthorn Cottage with a phone and a decision and a heart that was beating so hard she thought it might crack her ribs.

She looked at the phone. Callum's number was burned into her memory—she'd dialled it a thousand times, had seen it flash on her screen at all hours, had memorised it.

Her thumb hovered over the keypad.

This was it. The bridge. The crossing point. The moment when she either moved forward or stayed frozen in fear forever.

She thought about the flower path, about Emma's thoughts about it. Starting scared, growing brave, coming home. She thought about Joanna, who'd learned she deserved her own happiness.

She thought about Callum's face when

he'd proposed. The hope in it. The terror. The absolute certainty beneath both that she was what he wanted, who he wanted, forever if she'd have him.

And she thought about what he'd said: 'I love you. All of you. The flowers and the strangeness and the way you talk to birds. I love that you're magic. I love that you're real. I love you, Fern. Just as you are.'

She dialled the number.

It rang once. Twice. Three times.

'Hello?' His voice, uncertain, answering a number he didn't recognise.

'Callum.' Her own voice was barely a whisper. 'It's me.'

Silence. Then, 'Fern.' Not a question. Just her name, said like a prayer, like relief, like coming home.

'I'm sorry,' she said, and started to cry. 'I'm so sorry I ran. I was frightened. I'm still frightened. But I love you, and I'm a coward and an idiot, and I'm calling from a stranger's phone in a magical village where I've been living in a tent because I didn't know how to say yes when all I've ever wanted is to say yes, and—'

'Fern.' His voice was gentle, stopping her spiral. 'Breathe.'

She breathed.

'Are you okay?' he asked. 'Are you safe?'

'Yes. I'm in Lower Thistlewick. I'm camping. I'm reading stories to children. I'm leaving flowers everywhere, and everyone thinks I'm a fairy and—' She hiccupped a laugh through her tears. 'And I miss you so much I can't stand it.'

'I miss you too.' His voice was rough. 'I've been going mad. I thought— I thought I'd pushed too hard. Asked too soon. I was worried

I'd scared you away forever.'

'You didn't. I scared myself.' Fern wiped her eyes with the back of her hand. 'I'm not very brave, Callum. I run from things that matter. I'm not sure I know how to stop.'

'Then I'll come to you.' No hesitation. 'Where are you? Tell me the address, and I'll be there tomorrow.'

'You can't just—'

'I took this week off work just in case you called. I've been sitting by my phone all week, Fern. I can be there by noon tomorrow. Let me come. Let me see you. Let me—' His voice broke slightly. 'Let me try to convince you that you're worth waiting for.'

Fern looked around Hawthorn Cottage, at the warmth Joanna had built here, at the life she'd made after grief. She looked out the window at the garden, dormant but not dead, just waiting. She looked at her own reflection in the glass and saw a girl who was tired of running.

'Okay,' she said. 'Come tomorrow. I'll meet you on the bridge.'

'The bridge?'

'You'll see when you get here. It's where the magic lives.' She gave him directions to the village, to the green, to the bridge where this had all begun. 'Callum?'

'Yes?'

'I love you. I should have said it before. I should have said yes before. But I'm saying it now. I love you.'

'I love you too.' She could hear the smile in his voice. 'I'll see you tomorrow, Fern. On the magic bridge.'

After they hung up, Fern sat in Joanna's kitchen and cried properly—big, heaving sobs of relief and terror and hope all mixed together. When she finally emerged into the garden,

Joanna was pretending to inspect bare rose bushes, but looked up immediately.

'I called him,' Fern said.

'And?'

'He's coming tomorrow. He's going to try to convince me I'm worth waiting for.'

'And are you?' Joanna asked gently. 'Worth waiting for?'

Fern looked down at her feet. Small violets had bloomed around them while she'd been inside, pushing through the frost-hard ground. Evidence of magic. Evidence of life. Evidence of something in her that refused to stay dormant, no matter how scared she was.

'I think I might be,' she said. 'I think maybe I always was. I just had to come to a magical village and live in a tent and leave flowers everywhere before I could see it for myself.'

Joanna laughed and hugged her, and

Fern hugged her back, and in the distance, a robin sang as if celebrating.

Tomorrow, she would stand on the bridge and wait for Callum. Tomorrow, she would have to be brave. Tomorrow, everything would change.

But today, she was in a village that believed in magic, surrounded by people who thought her strangeness was a gift, learning slowly that deserving happiness wasn't something you earned—it was something you allowed.

Today, that was enough.

Chapter Eight

The Night Before

Fern couldn't sleep.

She lay in her tent listening to her own heartbeat, to the millstream's constant song, to the robin shifting on his perch near the tent pole. She'd called Callum. He was coming tomorrow. At noon, he'd be here, and she'd have to say all the things she'd been too frightened to say before.

What if she couldn't do it? What if she saw him and panicked again?

At three in the morning, she gave up on sleep entirely and crawled out of her tent into the February darkness. The village was completely silent—no lights in any windows, no sounds except the water and the wind in the bare trees. Even the robin stayed inside, tucked into warmth.

Fern walked to the bridge and sat on the wall, her legs dangling over the millstream, exactly where Emma had first found her. The moon was bright enough to read by, so she pulled out her mother's battered copy of *The Wind in the Willows* and opened it to a random page.

But instead of her mother's book, a photograph slipped out. The one Mrs Willoughby had given her—young Charlotte on this very bridge, laughing and hopeful and magical.

'What would you do?' Fern asked the photograph. 'If you were me right now, scared out of my mind, what would you do?'

The photograph didn't answer, obviously. But in her head, Fern could hear her mother's voice as clearly as if she'd been sitting beside her.

'I'd be brave, darling. Not because I wasn't frightened—I was always frightened. But because love is worth the fear. Every single time.'

Fern traced her mother's face in the photograph. Same hair. Same eyes. Same magic blooming around her feet, whether she meant it to or not.

'I don't know how to be as brave as you,' Fern whispered.

But that wasn't quite true, was it? She'd already done brave things. She'd come to this village. She'd let people see her magic. She'd called Callum. She'd said yes—or almost yes. She'd agreed to wait for him, to meet him, to try.

That was brave. Maybe not hero-brave, maybe not fairytale-brave, but brave in the quiet, ordinary way that mattered.

'Morning, fairy girl.'

Fern jumped, nearly dropping the photograph. Dimity was crossing the bridge towards her, wrapped in a thick coat and carrying two travel mugs.

'What are you doing up?' Fern asked.

'Couldn't sleep. Vivian said you probably couldn't either, so he made hot chocolate and sent me to find you.' Dimity handed over one of the mugs.

They sat together on the bridge wall, sipping chocolate that was exactly the right temperature, watching the moon reflected in the millstream.

'Today's the day,' Dimity said eventually. 'He arrives.'

'At noon. On this bridge.' Fern felt her stomach twist. 'I'm terrified.'

'Good. Fear means it matters.' Dimity shifted to face her properly. 'Can I tell you something? About when Vivian and I finally admitted we loved each other?'

Fern nodded.

'He'd left on Christmas Day. Said his agency called him back to Oxford—though that turned out to be a lie he told himself because he was frightened. We were apart for a week, and I was miserable. Convinced he'd left because he didn't love me. That I'd imagined everything between us.' Dimity's voice went soft. 'Then on New Year's Eve, my friend Lila drove up from London. She told me he was only twenty minutes away, renting a cottage in Burford. And that if I didn't go to him before midnight, I'd spend the whole new year regretting it.'

'So, you went?'

'I had to drive through a snowstorm on New Year's Eve to tell him. I was terrified he'd turn me away. That I'd knock on his door, and he'd tell me I'd misunderstood everything.' Dimity smiled at the memory. 'But I went anyway. Because the alternative—spending the rest of my life wondering "what if"—was worse than any rejection could be.'

'What happened when you got there?'

'He opened the door. And I told him he was a fool for leaving. That he'd made me believe my stories mattered, and then he'd disappeared before I could tell him that he mattered more.' Dimity squeezed Fern's hand. 'The courage wasn't in not being scared. It was in driving through that storm anyway. In knocking on that door, even though my hands were shaking.'

'What if he's changed his mind?' Fern asked, voicing her deepest fear. 'What if he's thought about it and realised I'm not worth the trouble?'

'Then you'll survive. You'll be heartbroken, but you'll survive. And you'll know you were brave enough to try.' Dimity's grip tightened. 'But I don't think he's changed his mind. I think he's been waiting, hoping, counting the days until you came back to him. Because that's what love does. It waits.'

They sat in silence for a while, two women who'd both faced their fears, both learning that courage was just another word for choosing love despite the terror.

'I should try to get a bit more sleep,' Fern said eventually. 'Today's going to be hard enough without me being exhausted.'

'Fair point.' Dimity slid off the bridge wall. 'But first—would you like help? Making yourself presentable for when he arrives?'

'Presentable?'

'You've been living in a tent for eight days. Your hair's in knots, you smell faintly of millstream, and I suspect you don't have anything clean to wear.' Dimity's tone was gentle, not critical. 'We could fix that. We could help you get ready.'

Tears pricked Fern's eyes. 'You'd do that?'

'Of course. That's what we do. We look after our own.' Dimity squeezed her shoulder. 'Sleep for a few hours. Then come to Pippin's Nook at eight. We'll take care of everything.'

After Dimity left, Fern returned to her tent and lay down, still clutching her mother's photograph. This time, exhaustion won over anxiety, and she fell into deep, dreamless sleep.

***

At eight o'clock, Fern knocked on the door of Pippin's Nook and found herself immediately swept inside by a gaggle of village women.

Dimity was there, obviously. But also Joanna, Mrs Pemberton from the village shop, Margaret from The Cosy Cup, and—to Fern's surprise—Emma, looking very serious and important.

'Right,' Dimity said, all business. 'Emma's in charge of hair. Joanna's got clothing sorted. Margaret brought breakfast. Mrs Pemberton's doing a manicure—your nails are disastrous, Fern, no offence. And I'm handling moral support and tea supply.'

'I don't—I mean—this is too much—' Fern stammered.

'Nonsense,' Mrs Pemberton said firmly. 'You're one of ours now. And we don't let one of ours face a marriage proposal looking like she's been dragged through a hedge backwards.'

'It's not a proposal,' Fern protested. 'He already proposed. I'm just—'

'Accepting it,' Joanna finished. 'Which is just as important. Possibly more important. First impressions matter.'

They sat Fern in a chair by the fire and

went to work. Emma washed and brushed her hair—'So much hair! And so tangled! This is going to take forever'—while Mrs Pemberton filed her nails and tutted over the state of her cuticles. Margaret pressed tea and toast into her hands, insisting she needed to eat properly. And Joanna laid out clothing options on the sofa.

'I brought three dresses from Hawthorn Cottage,' Joanna said. 'All roughly your size. You can't meet him in your flower dress, lovely as it is. You need something fresh.'

Fern looked at the dresses—a soft blue one, a sage green, and a deep plum. All simple, all beautiful, all far nicer than anything she'd brought with her.

'The green,' Emma said authoritatively, not looking up from hair-brushing. 'It matches your eyes. And it's romantic without being try-hard.'

'Very wise for twelve,' Dimity observed.

'I watch a lot of wedding shows,' Emma said seriously.

By ten o'clock, Fern had been transformed. Her hair fell in soft waves down her back, woven through with small purple flowers that Emma had insisted upon. Her nails were neat and clean. She was wearing Joanna's green dress, which fit perfectly, and Dimity had even found her a pair of pretty shoes instead of her battered trainers.

Dimity held up a mirror. 'Look.'

Fern looked and barely recognised herself. Not because she looked different, exactly, but because she looked... complete. Put together. Like a real person instead of a fairy tale that had wandered off the page.

'I look like I'm going to a wedding,' she said.

'Well, hopefully you will be soon,' Mrs Pemberton said. 'If that young man has any sense at all.'

'He has sense,' Emma said. 'I texted him. Joanna had his number from when you used her phone yesterday. He said he's been sitting by his phone all week waiting for you to call. That's very sensible behaviour for someone in love.'

'You texted him?' Fern couldn't decide if she was horrified or grateful.

'Someone had to make sure he was coming. I'm very responsible for my age.' Emma stood back, admiring her handiwork. 'There. You look perfect. Like a fairy who decided to be a real person for a day.'

'I am a real person,' Fern protested.

'You know what I mean.' Emma hugged her impulsively. 'You look happy. That's what I mean. You look like someone who's ready to say yes.'

The women all settled around the kitchen

table with fresh tea, and Joanna produced a tin of biscuits she'd made that morning. They sat together in comfortable companionship, these women who barely knew Fern but had taken her under their wing anyway.

'Thank you,' Fern said quietly. 'All of you. For this. For caring.'

'That's what community means,' Margaret said. 'Taking care of each other. Especially at the important moments.'

'My mother used to say that magic is just another word for being seen,' Joanna said softly. 'Really seen. Really known. Really loved anyway.' She looked at Fern. 'That's what we're doing. Seeing you. And loving you because of who you are, not despite it.'

Fern's vision blurred. 'I can't cry. Emma will kill me if I mess up my face.'

'Too right I will,' Emma said. 'I worked hard on that hair.'

At eleven-thirty, they walked Fern to the bridge. A small procession of women and one determined twelve-year-old, all bearing her up with their belief and care and absolute certainty that this was going to work out.

'He'll be here soon,' Dimity said, checking her watch. 'You should wait here. On the bridge. Where Emma first saw you. It's poetic.'

'It's terrifying,' Fern corrected.

'Both can be true.' Dimity hugged her quickly. 'You've got this. You're braver than you think.'

One by one, the women hugged her and retreated to a tactful distance—close enough to watch, far enough for privacy. Emma was last, squeezing Fern so hard she could barely breathe.

'Remember,' Emma whispered. 'Love is brave. You taught me that. Now you have to believe it yourself.'

Then Fern was alone on the bridge with the millstream flowing beneath her and the February sun climbing higher and her heart beating so hard she thought it might crack her ribs.

She looked down at her green dress, at the flowers in her hair, at the bridge beneath her feet. Looked across to the field where her tent had stood for more than a week. Looked at the path she'd worn with her walking, now fading as winter reclaimed its territory.

She thought about her mother standing in this exact spot thirty years ago, making the same choice. Running towards something instead of away. Choosing possible joy over certain loneliness.

'I can do this,' she whispered to herself, to her mother's memory, to the village that had taught her she was worth waiting for. *I can be brave.*

And then she heard it. The sound of a car pulling up in the lane. A door opening. Footsteps crossing the green.

Callum was here.

Fern took a deep breath, squared her shoulders, and waited on the bridge for her future to arrive.

Chapter Nine

The Language of Flowers

A man got out of the car—tall, dark-haired, rumpled from the drive, looking around at the village with obvious confusion. Then he saw the bridge, saw the flower path leading to it, and his whole face changed. Understanding. Wonder. The particular expression of someone who'd been told about magic and was now seeing it made real.

Then he saw Fern.

She stood up slowly, her legs shaking, her hands twisted together. Callum crossed the green towards her, and she could see his eyes taking her in—the flowers in her hair, her green dress, the tent in the field behind her, the evidence of eight days spent hiding from the thing she wanted most.

He stopped a few feet away.

'Hello, Fern,' he said, and his voice was exactly as she remembered. Warm. Steady. Home.

'Hello, Callum.' Her voice came out barely above a whisper.

They stared at each other for a long moment, and Fern was acutely aware of the women watching from their tactful distance. Of the village around them, holding its breath. Of the bridge behind her, waiting.

'I like your tent,' Callum said finally. 'Very fairy tale.'

'I've been living in it for eight days.'

'I gathered.' His smile was gentle, not mocking. 'Reading to children, Emma told me in approximately seven hundred text messages she sent to my number after getting it from your friend Joanna.'

'She's twelve. She's enthusiastic.'

'She said you've been leaving flowers everywhere.' He looked at the path, at the impossible blooms in February frost. 'She said the whole village thinks you're magic.'

'I'm not magic. I'm just—' Fern gestured helplessly at herself. 'I'm just me. Too strange and too scared and too—'

'Perfect.' Callum stepped closer. 'You're perfect, Fern. Exactly as you are. That's what I've been trying to tell you for a year. That's what I asked you to marry me for. Not despite the strangeness. Because of it. Because of all of it.'

'But what if—'

'What if nothing.' He was close enough now that Fern could see the shadows under his eyes, the evidence of a week of worry. 'What if I love you? What if that's enough? What if you stop asking "what if" and just let yourself be loved?'

Tears pricked Fern's eyes. 'I don't know how.'

'Then I'll teach you.' Callum reached out slowly, giving her time to pull away, and tucked one of the wildflowers more securely into her hair. 'We'll learn together. We'll be scared together. We'll make mistakes and fix them together. That's what marriage is, isn't it? Just promising to figure it out together, even when it's hard.'

'I ran away,' Fern said, as if he might have forgotten.

'I noticed.'

'I lived in a tent and read children's stories and hid from you like a complete coward.'

'I know.' His hand moved from her hair to cup her cheek. 'And I waited. Because I knew you'd come back. Because I knew you just needed time to believe what I've known all along—that you're worth waiting for. Worth fighting for. Worth everything.'

'Callum—'

'Marry me, Fern.' His voice was firm now, certain. 'Not someday. Not when you're ready. Now. Soon. As soon as we can arrange it. Marry me and let me spend the rest of my life proving you're loved.'

'I'm still scared,' she whispered.

'Good. Me too.' He smiled. 'Let's be scared together.'

And standing there on the village green, with flowers blooming around her feet and a robin singing from the bridge and people who barely knew her holding their breath in hope, Fern did the bravest thing she'd ever done.

She said yes.

Callum kissed her, and the village erupted in cheers. Emma shrieked with delight. Hugh and Joanna applauded. Doors opened all along the green as people came out to see what the noise was, found two young people embracing on the green, and started clapping too, without really knowing why.

When they finally broke apart, Fern was laughing and crying all at once, and Callum was looking at her like she was the answer to every question he'd ever had.

'Can I take down my tent now?' she asked.

'Definitely take down the tent.'

'And stop living like a romantic heroine on the run?'

'Please.'

'And maybe—' She took a deep breath. 'Maybe stay for a few more days? So you can meet the village properly? So they can know who you are before we leave?'

'We're not leaving until you're ready.' Callum glanced around at the village, at the impossible flowers, at the bridge that seemed to glow in the afternoon light. 'This place is magic. I can feel it. And if it helped you find your way back to me, then I owe it a proper thank you.'

Emma arrived then, launched herself at Callum with the confidence of a child who knew she'd made this happen, and informed him that he had to come to story time that afternoon because Fern was reading and it was the best thing ever, and also could he stay for dinner because Gran wanted to meet him.

Callum agreed to everything, looking slightly overwhelmed, and Fern loved him more than ever for just accepting it. For accepting her village, her magic, her strangeness. For accepting all of her.

That afternoon, Fern read from *The Wind in the Willows*—the chapter where Mole finds his old home and realises that home isn't just a place but the people who welcome you back. Callum sat at the back, holding Emma's hand because the child had claimed him immediately, and watched Fern bring the story to life. When she reached the part where Mole catches the scent of his old home—where he realises that home isn't about the place but about being welcomed and loved—Fern looked up and met Callum's eyes across the assembled children. He smiled at her, and she smiled back, and it was a promise. That they would make each other Real. That they would choose love even when it was frightening. That they would cross every bridge together, hand in hand.

After the reading, after dinner at The Old Swan, where Callum charmed everyone without trying, after a walk along the millstream path with Dimity and Vivian, who wanted to congratulate them personally, Fern and Callum stood together on the bridge.

'This is where Emma first saw me,' Fern said. 'She thought I was a fairy. She was sitting there—' She pointed to the wall. 'And I was sitting here, reading. And everything was about to change, but I didn't know it yet.'

'And now?' Callum pulled her close, wrapping his arms around her against the February cold.

'Now I know.' Fern leaned into him, into his warmth, into the solid reality of being loved. 'Now I'm ready to cross.'

They stood on the bridge for a long time, watching the millstream flow beneath them, quiet and constant and sure. Tomorrow, they would pack up Fern's tent. They would say goodbye to the village that had taught her she was worth waiting for. They would drive home together and start planning a wedding.

But tonight, they were exactly where they needed to be—standing on a bridge between one life and another.

Together.

Beneath them, the millstream sang its ancient song. Around them, spring flowers bloomed. Above them, a robin settled on the bridge rail and kept watch.

And on the bridge in Lower Thistlewick, on a February evening when spring felt close despite the frost, two people chose to believe in happy endings.

Sometimes that was all the magic required.

Chapter Ten

Valentine's Day

They didn't leave that night after all.

Mrs Willoughby had invited them to dinner—"a proper family dinner, now that we're being honest"—and one dinner had led to tea at Pippin's Nook with Dimity and Vivian, which had led to a promise to attend Sunday service at the village church "just to see it", which somehow meant they were still in Lower Thistlewick when Valentine's morning arrived.

Fern woke in the guest room at Mrs Willoughby's cottage—a proper bed at last, after a week of camping—with Callum in the room next door because Mrs Willoughby was old-fashioned about such things.

'Valentine's Day,' Mrs Willoughby announced at breakfast, setting down a plate of heart-shaped pancakes. 'Special day for lovers.

The village always celebrates properly.'

'We should probably head home soon,' Fern started, but Callum shook his head.

'One more day won't hurt. Besides, I want to see how a magical village celebrates Valentine's Day.' He caught Fern's eye and smiled. 'Humour me?'

So they stayed.

***

By nine o'clock, the village green had been transformed. Paper hearts hung from tree to tree. Children ran about with red ribbons. Margaret from The Cosy Cup had set up a table with heart-shaped biscuits and hot chocolate, and someone had arranged hay bales in a circle for seating.

'It's like something from a fairy tale,' Callum said, slightly awed.

'Everything here is like a fairy tale,' Emma corrected, appearing at his elbow. She was wearing a red jumper with hearts painted on her cheeks. 'Come on, we're making valentines for everyone.'

She dragged them to a table where children and adults alike were cutting paper, writing messages, decorating cards with the intense concentration of people who took Valentine's Day seriously.

Hugh and Joanna were already there, working on a card together. Dimity and Vivian sat close, their heads bent over a shared piece of paper. Even Tom from the pub was cutting out a lopsided heart with surprising accuracy.

'This one's for you and Callum,' Emma said, presenting them with a wobbly heart decorated with flowers and birds. Inside, in careful letters: *To Fern and Callum, thank you for showing me that love is brave. Love, Emma.*

Fern blinked away tears. 'That's so

beautiful.'

'You were brave,' Emma said seriously. 'You ran away, and then you came back. That's the hardest kind of brave.'

They spent the morning making valentines, drinking hot chocolate, and watching the village come alive with celebration. Callum fit in seamlessly, laughing with Hugh about the challenges of raising daughters, helping the younger children with their scissors work, and charming Mrs Pemberton by complimenting her jam.

'He's a keeper,' Dimity murmured to Fern. 'You chose well.'

'He chose me first,' Fern pointed out.

'Love isn't about who chose first. It's about choosing each other every day.' Dimity watched Vivian across the green, showing a group of children a complicated paper-folding technique. 'Every morning, I wake up and choose him. And he chooses me. That's what makes it work.'

***

At noon, Hugh announced that everyone was invited to Chapter & Verse for a special Valentine's reading—love poetry, adults welcome.

The bookshop was filled with couples of all ages: Hugh and Joanna, Dimity and Vivian, the elderly Pembertons holding hands after fifty-three years of marriage, young parents with babies, and teenagers looking nervous and hopeful.

And Fern and Callum, sitting together in the wingback chair by the fire—Callum in the seat, Fern perched on the arm, his hand resting on her waist.

Hugh had selected the poems carefully. Shakespeare's Sonnet 116, Elizabeth Barrett Browning's *How Do I Love Thee.*' Also, Mary

Oliver's '*Wild Geese.*' Pieces about love that endured, love that transformed, love that accepted you exactly as you were.

When it was Fern's turn to read—because of course everyone expected it—she chose E.E. Cummings: *i carry your heart with me (i carry it in my heart)*.

Her voice caught on the words "here is the deepest secret nobody knows", but Callum's hand tightened on her waist, steadying her. She finished the poem, closed the book, and looked down at him.

'That's how I love you,' she said quietly, aware that the entire bookshop was listening but not caring. 'I carry your heart with me. I've been carrying it since the day we met. Even when I ran, I was carrying it. I just had to learn that carrying someone's heart isn't a burden. It's a gift.'

Callum stood, pulled her properly into

his arms, and kissed her in front of the entire village.

Everyone applauded. Emma cheered. Mrs Pemberton declared it the most romantic thing she'd seen in sixty years. And Fern, wrapped in Callum's arms, surrounded by a village that had taught her about courage and magic and love, was completely, utterly happy.

****

That afternoon, they walked along the millstream together, needing space from the village's beautiful chaos.

The flower path was fading now—Fern hadn't walked it in days—but traces remained. Stubborn violets. Primroses refusing to die. Snowdrops that might have been natural or might have been magic.

'What are you thinking?' Callum asked.

'That I'm happy.' Fern tested the words and found them true. 'Properly happy. Not waiting for disaster. Just... happy.'

'Good.' He pulled her close. 'You deserve to be happy.'

'I'm starting to believe that.'

They stood on their bridge and watched the millstream rush past, higher today after overnight rain but still constant, still sure of its path.

'When we get back to London,' Callum said, 'we should start planning properly. The wedding. Where we'll live.'

'Your flat or mine?'

'Neither. Let's find somewhere new. Somewhere that's ours together.' He turned her to face him. 'Somewhere with a garden. So you can grow things.'

'Flowers grow whether I want them to or not.'

'But you should have a garden anyway. A place that's yours. Where you can be as magical as you want.' Callum kissed her forehead. 'I want to build a life with you. Not slot you into my existing life but build something new together.'

'That's very romantic for an accountant.'

'Perfect.' Callum pulled her closer. 'Though I'd marry you tomorrow if you asked.'

'Let's give it a few months. Let me finish my degree. Let us settle into the flat to begin with.' Fern smiled. 'Besides, Emma needs time to plan. She's already organising the whole thing in her head, I can tell.'

***

That evening, the village gathered on the green for music and dancing. Someone had brought a fiddle, someone else a guitar, and Hugh contributed a record player with a stack of old vinyl.

Soon, the February night was filled with music and laughter and the joy of people who'd chosen to celebrate love in all its forms.

Fern and Callum danced on the green under the fairy lights someone had strung from the trees. They weren't good dancers—Fern kept stepping on his feet, and Callum had no rhythm whatsoever—but they were happy.

Around them, the village danced too. Hugh and Joanna moved together with the ease of new love. Dimity and Vivian waltzed like they'd done it a thousand times. The elderly Pembertons showed everyone how it was done. Emma danced with her friends, then with her father, and then with Callum when he offered his hand.

And on the bridge, the robin watched. And in the cottages, the magic hummed. And beneath it all, the millstream flowed, carrying old stories downstream as new stories were created.

This was what love looked like, Fern

thought. Full of music and laughter and people who were there because they cared.

When the dancing finally ended, and the village began to disperse, they walked with Mrs Willoughby back to her cottage. They sat by her fire, exhausted and content as she brought hot chocolate.

'Thank you,' Fern said quietly. 'For everything. For being family. For helping me find my courage.'

'You always had courage, dear girl. You just needed to remember where you'd left it.' Mrs Willoughby patted her hand. 'Your mother would be very proud.'

Callum cleared his throat. 'Mrs Willoughby, I have a question. If Fern and I get married in the spring—here in the village, on the bridge or the green—would you... Would you stand with Fern and her father?'

Mrs Willoughby's eyes filled with tears.

'Charlotte would have wanted me to stand in for her. And I am honoured to accept.'

Callum pulled Fern close as she shed a tear, and Mrs Willoughby poured more hot chocolate with shaking hands.

Later, walking, Fern paused on the bridge one more time.

'Happy Valentine's Day,' Callum said.

'Best one ever,' Fern replied.

'Really? Better than last year when I burned dinner, and we had toast?'

'Much better. Because last year, I still thought you might wake up and realise you'd made a mistake. This year, I know you won't.'

'Never,' Callum promised. 'Not in a million years.'

They kissed goodnight on the bridge, and somewhere beneath them, new snowdrops bloomed in the cracks between stones—small and perfect and full of promise.

Chapter Eleven

Belonging

Callum and Fern stayed four more days.

On Monday, they helped Hugh reorganise the children's section at Chapter & Verse. Callum proved surprisingly good at building shelves, and Fern created a reading nook in the corner—cushions, blankets and fairy lights that made it feel like stepping into a story.

'This is perfect,' Hugh said, standing back to admire their work. 'Emma's going to love it.'

'It's the least we could do,' Fern said. 'After everything you've done for us.'

'We haven't done anything except be here.' Hugh smiled. 'That's how the village works. We just show up for each other.'

That afternoon, they read to the children in the new nook. Fern read, but this time Callum helped—holding up pictures, doing voices for different characters, making the children laugh. And Fern, watching him with a six-year-old on his lap, felt her heart swell.

He was going to be a wonderful father someday. If they decided they wanted children. And watching him here, so natural and easy with kids, Fern thought maybe they would.

On Tuesday, they helped Joanna in the garden at Hawthorn Cottage. It was still too early for serious planting, but there was pruning to do, beds to prepare, and bulbs to check.

'I've never been good with gardens,' Callum admitted, wielding pruning shears with more enthusiasm than skill. 'My mum always said I had black thumbs.'

'You're doing fine,' Joanna assured him. 'And besides, with Fern around, everything grows whether you're skilled or not.'

It was true. Where Fern walked in the garden, tiny green shoots appeared. Nothing dramatic—just the first hints of spring coming early. Crocuses pushing through. Daffodils preparing to bloom. The sleeping garden waking up because she was there.

'You really are magic,' Callum said, watching a primrose unfurl beside where Fern was kneeling.

'Or the garden just likes me.' But Fern was smiling.

They worked through the afternoon, and Hugh joined them after closing the shop, and soon it became less about gardening and more about conversation.

Hugh talked about Sarah, his first wife, and the grief that had nearly destroyed him and Emma both. About how the village had held them together when they couldn't hold themselves.

'I didn't think I'd ever be happy again,' he admitted. 'Didn't think I deserved to be. Sarah was my person, and when she died, I thought that was it. My one chance at love, gone.'

'But then Joanna came after a few years,' Fern said softly.

'But then Joanna came.' Hugh looked at Joanna with such love that Fern had to look away. 'And the village showed me that love isn't finite. That opening your heart again doesn't diminish what came before. It just makes room for more.'

Callum squeezed Fern's hand. 'I'm glad you didn't give up on love.'

'I'm glad you didn't give up on me,' Fern replied.

On Wednesday, they helped at The Cosy Cup. Margaret needed extra hands during the breakfast rush, and Fern found herself waiting tables while Callum worked the coffee machine under Margaret's exacting supervision.

'Not too much foam!' Margaret called. 'The locals don't like too much foam!'

'Yes, ma'am,' Callum said, grinning.

The morning was chaos—orders shouted, plates balanced, the constant hiss of the espresso machine. But it was also happy. Villagers called out greetings. Children ate biscuits when their parents weren't looking.

During a lull, Alf came in from the pub and sat at the counter. 'Heard you two are sticking around a while.'

'Few more days,' Callum said, pouring him coffee. 'Hard to leave.'

'Always is. Village has a way of grabbing hold.' Alf added sugar to his coffee—three heaped spoons. 'My wife and I, we came here thirty years ago for a weekend. Never left.'

'Never?' Fern asked.

'Never saw the point. Everything we needed was here. Community, purpose, magic.' Alf sipped his coffee and nodded approval at Callum. 'You'll be back. Both of you. Village doesn't let go once it's claimed you.'

'Is that good or bad?' Callum asked.

'Yes,' Alf said, and laughed at his own joke.

On Thursday, they helped with the village's community outreach program—visiting elderly residents who couldn't leave their homes easily. Mrs Pemberton organised it, arriving at Mrs Willoughby's cottage with a list and a basket of supplies.

'Mr Henderson needs his groceries delivered. Mrs Clark likes company for tea. Old Tom—not pub Tom, the other Tom—needs help changing his light bulbs.' She handed Fern the basket. 'Think you can manage?'

'Of course,' Fern said.

They spent the day visiting people Fern had never met. Mr Henderson, who told them about the beautiful garden he once had. Mrs Clark, who taught them a card game and served them tea in delicate china cups. Old Tom, who turned out to be ninety-three and insisted on climbing the ladder himself despite Callum's protests.

'I'm not dead yet,' he said. 'And I'll change my own damn light bulbs until I am.'

But he let Callum spot him, and afterwards they sat in his garden—dormant now but clearly loved—and he told them about his wife who'd died ten years ago.

'She was magic, my Norma. Made things grow just by looking at them.' He glanced at Fern. 'Like you, I reckon. Heard about the flowers you've been leaving everywhere.'

'I don't mean to,' Fern said.

'Best things never are meant. They just are.' Old Tom smiled.

That night, before they went to bed at Mrs Willoughby's cottage—they'd moved Callum into the spare room next door, propriety be damned—Fern thought about their day.

'I like it here,' she said into the darkness. 'I like being part of something. Mattering to people.'

From the next room, Callum's voice came through the wall. 'Then we'll come back often. As often as you want. This can be our second home.'

'Promise?'

'Promise.'

On Friday, they helped Emma with her school project. It involved an alarming amount of glitter, a papier-mâché colosseum, and Callum reading from a textbook about Julius Caesar in a terrible Italian accent that made

Emma giggle helplessly.

'You're terrible at this,' she said, still laughing.

'I'm an accountant, not an actor,' Callum protested.

'You're terrible at being an accountant too,' Fern teased. 'You haven't checked your work email all week.'

'Because I'm on holiday.' But Callum looked sheepish. 'Should I check it?'

'Absolutely not,' Hugh said, coming into the room with tea. 'You're learning the first rule of the village: when you're here, you're here, and the world can wait.'

They finished Emma's project around dinnertime—the colosseum resplendent with glitter, the essay typed up neatly, the whole thing ready to impress her teachers.

'You're the best,' Emma said, hugging them both. 'Can you come to parents' evening and pretend to be my parents? Dad's great, but having the girl who makes magic happen and her fancy accountant fiancé would be so much cooler.'

'I'd love that,' Fern said.

'Good.' Emma squeezed tighter. 'Because you're family now, you know. That means you have to visit lots.' Her expression turned serious. 'You are coming back, right? For the wedding, at least?'

'For the wedding,' Fern promised. 'And before that. Easter, maybe. To check on the snowdrops.'

'And summer,' Emma pressed. 'And Christmas. And whenever you're sad and need reminding that you're loved.'

'All of those times,' Callum agreed. 'You're stuck with us now.'

'Good,' Emma said, satisfied. 'That's how it's supposed to be.'

***

That evening, their last evening before leaving, the village threw them a farewell dinner at The Old Swan. Nothing formal—just everyone crowded into the pub, sharing food and stories and laughter.

Alf made another terrible joke: 'Why did the fairy and the accountant make a good couple? Because one was magic and the other knew how to budget for it!'

Mrs Willoughby stood and raised her glass. 'To Fern and Callum. Who came to us separately and are leaving together. May your life together be full of magic and joy with flowers in unexpected places.'

'To Fern and Callum!' the pub chorused.

Fern smiled and laughed all evening. These people had taught her she was worth loving and shown her what it meant to belong.

'Thank you,' she said. 'All of you. For

everything.'

'That's what family does,' Dimity called from her corner. 'We show up.'

'And we'll keep showing up,' Vivian added. 'Whenever you need us.'

Later, walking back to Mrs Willoughby's cottage, Fern and Callum stopped on the bridge. Their bridge. The place where everything had begun and, in a way, where everything would begin again when they came back for their wedding.

'Are you ready to leave?' Callum asked.

Fern looked around at the village sleeping under stars, at the cottages with their glowing windows, at the millstream flowing dark and constant beneath them.

'Yes,' she said. 'Because I know we'll come back. And because I'm not running anymore. I'm just... going home. With you.'

'Home,' Callum repeated, testing the

word. 'I like the sound of that.'

'So do I.'

They kissed on the bridge one last time, and where their feet touched the stone, tiny white flowers bloomed—snowdrops, perfect and impossible, full of promise.

Chapter Twelve

The Leaving Day

They left on a grey Tuesday morning, ten days after Valentine's Day, when February was beginning to soften at its edges and hint at spring.

Fern woke early in Mrs Willoughby's guest room and lay for a moment listening to the sounds of the village waking up: birds singing, the millstream's constant song, someone opening a door down the lane. The quiet of a village where everyone knew everyone, and where nothing much changed.

She was going to miss it desperately.

Callum was already awake in the room next door—she could hear him moving about, packing. They'd stayed longer than planned, neither quite ready to leave this place that had brought their happiness. But real life was waiting. Jobs and flats and all the practical considerations of building a future together.

She dressed quickly and went downstairs to find Mrs Willoughby already in the kitchen making breakfast.

'There's my girl,' her great-aunt said, pulling her into a hug. 'Last morning in the village. How are you feeling?'

'Ready,' Fern said, surprised to find it was true. 'Scared. Happy. All of it at once.'

'That sounds about right.' Mrs Willoughby set a plate of toast on the table. 'Sit. Eat. You've got a long drive ahead.'

They ate together, and Fern thought about how strange it was that she hadn't known her great-aunt existed. Now Mrs Willoughby felt like family in the truest sense—someone who'd seen her at her worst and loved her anyway.

'I'll visit,' Fern said. 'Often. I promise.'

'I know you will. You have Willoughby blood. We always come home eventually.' Mrs Willoughby poured more tea. 'Your mother did. Ran here when she needed courage, went back when she found it. History repeating itself, in the best possible way.'

'Do you think she'd be proud of me? For finally saying yes?'

'I think she'd be cross it took you so long.' But Mrs Willoughby's smile was gentle. 'And yes, darling. Enormously proud. You came here frightened, and you're leaving brave. That's all any mother could want for her child.'

Callum appeared in the doorway, dressed for travel, looking rumpled yet perfect. Mrs Willoughby immediately stood and began loading another plate with breakfast.

'Sit,' she commanded. 'You don't leave this house without a proper meal inside you.'

***

By nine o'clock, they'd packed Callum's car with Fern's rucksack, her tent, and bags of gifts the village had pressed upon them. Books from Hugh. Jam from Mrs Pemberton. A watercolour of the bridge from Joanna. A beautiful leather journal from Dimity with a note tucked inside, *For writing your own story. Choose happy endings.*

The robin sat on the car roof, apparently supervising the packing process.

'You know he's coming with us, don't you?' Callum said, eyeing the bird.

'He's wild. He'll stay here where he belongs.'

But when she said it, the robin chirped—a sound that seemed distinctly sceptical—and Fern laughed despite herself.

They'd said most of their goodbyes the

night before at The Old Swan. But there were still a few people waiting on the green when they emerged from Mrs Willoughby's cottage. Dimity and Vivian, holding hands. Hugh was with Emma, who was wearing her school uniform and trying not to cry. A scattering of villagers who'd come to wave them off.

'You'll come back? Promise?' Emma asked, when Fern knelt to hug her goodbye.

'Definitely. How else will I know how your Romans project turns out?'

'Promise?'

'Promise.' Fern squeezed her tight. 'Thank you for knowing who I was before I knew myself.'

'You're still a fairy,' Emma whispered. 'Even in London. Don't forget.'

'I won't.'

Dimity hugged her next, quick and warm. 'Call if you need anything. Advice, encouragement, someone to tell you that being strange is wonderful. Anything.'

'Thank you. For everything. For understanding.'

'We strange girls have to stick together.' Dimity pulled back, her eyes bright. 'Be happy, Fern. You deserve it.'

Vivian hugged her too, then Joanna, then Hugh. A chain of embraces and good wishes and people who barely knew her but had adopted her anyway.

Mrs Willoughby was last, holding Fern at arm's length and studying her face.

'You look different from when you arrived,' she said. 'Lighter. Like you've put down something heavy you'd been carrying too long.'

'I have.' Fern could feel tears threatening. 'I don't know how to thank you. For everything. For being family. For giving me space to figure out my heart.'

'You don't thank family. You just love them.' Mrs Willoughby kissed her cheek. 'Now go. Live your extraordinary ordinary life. Fall in love with Callum a little more every day. Grow flowers wherever you go. Be exactly who you are and never apologise for it.'

'I'll try.'

'You'll succeed.' Mrs Willoughby turned to Callum. 'Take care of her.'

'Always,' he promised.

'Good. Because if you don't, you'll answer to me. And I'm old and mean, and I know where you live.'

Callum laughed and hugged her too, this elderly woman he'd known for less than two weeks who'd nevertheless become important to them both.

They got in the car—Fern in the passenger seat, Callum behind the wheel. The robin immediately flew down and settled on the dashboard, as if this had been the plan all along.

'I told you,' Callum said.

'Apparently he's coming to London.' Fern looked at the robin, at this small piece of village magic that had decided to follow them home. 'Well. All right then. Welcome to the city.'

They drove slowly away from Mrs Willoughby's cottage, past the field where Fern's tent had stood. Past Hawthorn Cottage, where Joanna waved from the window. Past Chapter & Verse, where Hugh was opening up for the day. Past Pippin's Nook, where Dimity and Vivian stood in their doorway, arms around each other.

And finally, past the bridge.

Fern turned in her seat to look at it as they drove away. The stone bridge where Emma had first found her. Where she'd read stories to children. Where she'd talked with Dimity about fear and courage. Where she'd stood with Callum and decided to be brave.

The bridge where everything had changed.

'Goodbye,' she whispered.

And perhaps it was her imagination, or perhaps it was the village's particular magic, but she could have sworn she saw new snowdrops blooming in the cracks between the stones.

***

They drove in silence for a while, leaving the Cotswolds behind, heading toward London and their real life. The robin dozed on the dashboard. The countryside rolled past, brown fields giving way to towns giving way to the slow creep of the city.

'Nervous?' Callum asked as they hit the outskirts of London.

'Excited,' Fern said, realising it was true. 'Ready to start our life.'

'Good. Because I found us a new flat.'

Fern turned to stare at him. 'What? When?'

'Yesterday, while you were helping Joanna in her garden. I called the estate agent about that Camberwell place we liked—the one with the garden, and they said the previous applicants had fallen through. So, I said we'd take it.' He glanced at her, suddenly uncertain. 'Was that too presumptuous? Should I have asked you first?'

'No.' Fern reached over and took his hand. 'It's perfect. When can we move in?'

'This weekend. If we want it.'

'We want it.'

They grinned at each other; this was real. This was happening.

'We should set a date,' Callum said. 'For

the wedding.'

'Spring,' Fern said immediately. 'In the village. On the bridge, maybe, or on the green. Somewhere outside, somewhere the flowers can bloom even if they're not supposed to.'

'Spring it is.' Callum lifted her hand and kissed it.

They merged onto the motorway, London growing larger ahead of them. 'What do you think happens next? For the village, I mean.'

'Someone else arrives who needs it.' Fern said it with certainty. 'That's what Mrs Willoughby said. The village waits, and watches, and when the right person comes—someone broken or scared or running—it helps them. That's what it does.'

'Do you think they'll be as magical as you?'

'Everyone's magical in their own way.

They'll have their own story.' Fern looked out the window at the city appearing on the horizon. 'And the village will help them write a happy ending, just like it did for me.'

'For us,' Callum corrected.

'For us,' Fern agreed.

***

They spent the afternoon at Callum's flat—soon to be former flat—making lists and plans. Where their furniture would go in the new place. What they needed to buy. When they'd visit the village again—Easter, they decided, to check on the snowdrops and see how Emma's Romans project had turned out.

The robin explored the flat with great interest, eventually settling on a potted basil plant by the window as if claiming it as his new territory.

'We need to name him,' Callum said, watching the bird preen its feathers.

'You can't name a wild bird.'

'He's not wild. He's domesticated now. He lives with us. He needs a name.'

Fern considered the robin, who looked back at her with what seemed like expectation. 'What about Willoughby? After Great-Aunt Iris?'

'Perfect. Will for short.'

'Will the Robin,' Fern said, trying it out. 'All right. Welcome home, Will.'

The robin chirped approval and went back to investigating the basil plant.

That evening, they walked to the Camberwell flat to measure rooms and dream about furniture placement. The garden was bare and brown in the February cold, but Fern could see its potential. Where roses would climb. Where herbs would flourish. Where they'd sit on summer evenings and watch the sunset.

'I'll plant it in spring,' she said, standing

in the middle of the small plot. 'Properly. With intention. Not just flowers that appear because I'm walking somewhere.'

'Both kinds of flowers are nice,' Callum said. 'The intentional and the accidental.'

'I suppose that's true of most things.' Fern looked up at the flat—their flat, with its two bedrooms and its kitchen window that looked over the garden. 'This is really happening, isn't it? We're really doing this.'

'We are.' Callum wrapped his arms around her from behind. 'Scared?'

'Not anymore.' And it was true. 'I learned something in the village.'

'What's that?'

'That magic isn't something outside yourself. It's just being brave enough to believe you deserve good things.' Fern leaned back into him. 'I deserve this. We deserve this. And I'm going to spend every day being grateful for it.'

'Good.' Callum kissed the top of her head. 'Because I plan to spend every day making sure you never forget that.'

They stood in their soon-to-be garden as twilight fell, wrapped in each other and their plans and the happiness that came from knowing you were exactly where you belonged.

Tomorrow they'd start moving. Tomorrow, real life would begin in earnest. Tomorrow, they'd start building the extraordinary ordinary life Mrs Willoughby had wished for them.

But tonight, they had this—each other, a garden waiting for spring, and the quiet certainty that they'd crossed the bridge and chosen the right direction.

***

That night, Fern couldn't sleep. She lay in Callum's bed—their bed now, technically, since they'd be married soon and it seemed silly to maintain separate flats in the meantime—and thought about everything that had changed in eight days away from him.

'I love you,' Callum murmured sleepily.

'I love you too.'

Fern closed her eyes and felt herself drifting toward sleep, peaceful and exactly where she belonged. Tomorrow would bring the chaos of moving house.

But tonight, she was home with the man she loved.

And somewhere three hours away, in a Cotswold village that knew exactly what its residents needed, an old stone bridge waited patiently for the next person who would need its particular magic. The millstream flowed. The cottages kept watch. And the village settled into sleep, content in the knowledge that it had done its job once more.

Another broken heart healed. Another

lost soul found. Another story given its happy ending.

And in the cracks of the bridge, snowdrops bloomed—small and perfect and full of promise.

Magic, the village whispered to itself. Or just love, believed in completely.

THE END

March Magic: … coming in March

Ten years of marriage.

Ten years of hope, disappointment, and the slow, silent drift that comes when every month brings fresh heartbreak. Sophie and Daniel Ashford thought a fresh start in the Cotswolds might save them—a sabbatical, a break from the constant medical appointments and whispered apologies.

Just six months in Violet Cottage to remember why they fell in love. But Violet Cottage has other plans. A tender story of marriage, grief, and the courage it takes to start again with the person you thought you'd lost.

Available in eBook:
http://books2read.com/u/4Eqd70

Available for print pre-order in Annie's store:
https://annieseatonstore.ecwid.com/March-Magic-Enchanted-Village-Book-4-Pre-order-March-p803861302

Also by Annie Seaton

Daughters of the Darling
From Across the Sea
Over the River
By the Billabong
Beneath Still Waters
Under Darling Skies

A Bec Whitfield Mystery
Bowen River
Shadows on the Shore
Storm Season
Dark Waters

Enchanted Village Series
A Magic Christmas
January Joy
February Frolics
March Magic
Mayday Magic
Midsummer Magic
Harvest Magic

The Catherine Snowden Series
The Forest Keeps
The Drowning Hour

The Happy Outback Hotel (2026)
Outback Strangers
Outback Secrets
Outback Dreams
Outback Hearts

Outback Spirit
Outback Promise
Outback Horizon
Outback Silence
Outback Whispers
Outback Flame

Duckinwilla Days
Coming Home
Secrets and Surprises
Wishes and Whispers
Chasing Dreams
New Beginnings
All Together Now

Home to the Outback
Lucy
Angie
Jemima
Isabella

Porter Sisters Series
Kakadu Sunset
Daintree
Diamond Sky
Hidden Valley
Larapinta
Kakadu Dawn

Others
Whitsunday Dawn
Undara
Osprey Reef
East of Alice
One Summer in Tuscany
Four Seasons Short and Sweet

Follow the Sun
Ten Days in Paradise
Deadly Secrets
Adventures in Time
Silver Valley Witch
The Emerald Necklace
A Clever Christmas
Christmas with the Boss
Her Christmas Star
The Emerald Necklace

The Augathella Girls Series
Outback Roads
Outback Sky
Outback Escape
Outback Wind
Outback Dawn
Outback Moonlight
Outback Dust
Outback Hope
Boxed Sets
Augathella Girls 1-4
Augathella Girls 5-8
Augathella Short and Sweet Series
An Augathella Surprise
An Augathella Baby
An Augathella Spring
An Augathella Christmas
An Augathella Wedding
An Augathella Easter
An Augathella Masquerade Ball
Boxed Sets
Augathella Short and Sweet 1-3
Augathella Short and Sweet 1-4

Sunshine Coast Series
Waiting for Ana
The Trouble with Jack
Healing His Heart
Sunshine Coast Boxed Set

The Richards Brothers Series
The Trouble with Paradise
Marry in Haste
Outback Sunrise
Richards Brothers Boxed Set

Bondi Beach Love Series
Beach House
Beach Music
Beach Walk
Beach Dreams
The House on the Hill_Boxed Set

Second Chance Bay Series
Her Outback Playboy
Her Outback Protector
Her Outback Haven
Her Outback Paradise
The McDougalls of Second Chance Bay_Boxed Set

Love Across Time Series
Come Back to Me
Follow Me
Finding Home
The Threads that Bind
Love Across Time 1-4 Boxed Set

Bindarra Creek Series
Worth the Wait
Full Circle

FEBRUARY FROLICS

Secrets of River Cottage
A Clever Christmas
A Place to Belong
Hearts in Harmony

Secrets of River Cottage

Awards

2024: Finalist - Romantic suspense category, RUBY award for *From Across the Sea*.

2023: Winner - Long contemporary novel category, RUBY award for *Larapinta*.

2023: Finalist - Australian Romance Readers Awards for *Kakadu Dawn,* the sixth and final book in the Porter Sisters series.
2018 and 2020: Finalist - for the NZ KORU Award.

2017: Winner - Best Established Author of the Year 2017 AUSROM

2017: Winner - Author of the Year 2014 AUSROM
Best Established Author, AUSROM Readers' Choice.

2016, 2017, 2018, 2019: Longlisted - Sisters in Crime Davitt Awards

2016: Finalist - Book of the Year, Long Romance, RWA Ruby Awards for *Kakadu Sunset*

2015: Winner - Best Established Author of the Year AUSROM